A DISGRACE TO HER COUNTRY

EH-99

A DISGRACE
TO HER COUNTRY

Peter Young

The Book Guild Ltd
Sussex, England

The Book Guild Ltd,
25 High Street,
Lewes, Sussex

First published 1997
© Peter Young 1997

Set in Times
Typesetting by
CentraCet, Cambridge

Printed in Great Britain by
Bookcraft (Bath) Ltd, Avon

A catalogue record for this book is
available from the British Library

ISBN 1 85776 231 2

*Many thanks to Chris McCullum for
help with the manuscript
Dedicated to my devoted wife Galina*

CONTENTS

FOREWORD

It is a deep pleasure and honour to write a foreword to this book by Peter Young. I only came to know Peter and Galina, a remarkable couple, long after the events described in this fascinating book. Much that I read here was new to me, although I had heard them talk of some of the episodes in their dramatic story of the mid and late 1970s.

Peter Young writes movingly about his meeting in Zambia with the young Russian teacher, Galina. They fell in love and endured stress and privation beyond the experience and imagination of many before their story was happily resolved. Their drama reminds one of a world that is now, with the passing of Soviet Communism, all but dead. Peter's and Galina's own exodus is a story of hope and of triumph of love and the human spirit over a repressive state regime, which was afraid to let people think and act for themselves.

A Disgrace To Her Country deserves to be read widely. It is the true story of two unusually determined people and their discovery of freedom and happiness together.

Anthony Seldon

PROLOGUE

Senanga, Zambia: October 1975

'Galina – you've forgotten your propaganda!'

I'd noticed how absent-minded this new teacher seemed to be, always leaving magazines and booklets lying around the staffroom. She'd just dropped a pile of what looked like travel brochures on the table, so I shouted after her. It was meant to be a joke, but when she came back her face was white as chalk.

I gathered up the stuff she'd left. She took it without a word and ran out of the room. Far from raising a smile, my not very subtle quip had misfired. She was obviously upset, and her reaction intrigued me.

I didn't know much about Galina Vasilyeva. I'd sorted out her timetable the day she arrived, and given her a quick tour of the school, all part of my duties as an established member of the maths department, which Galina was joining. She had listened attentively, and now and then she'd say, 'Please speak more slowly.' Otherwise she hardly said a word to me.

For months we'd been hearing rumours about Russian teachers coming to Senanga.

I had been teaching in Zambia for seven years and had got used to hearing speculation about the Russians mounting an 'attack' on Africa. According to rumour in the expatriate community, phase one of the plan was to establish personnel in Zambia, especially in the education sphere.

From what I heard, the aim was first to convince the people they were being exploited by the West, then to indoctrinate

1

them into Communism without any obvious pushing of ideas. They were working ten years ahead, hoping the eventual turn-round in allegiance would look as though it came from the Zambians themselves.

I've never been much of a political animal, and none of this interested me all that much at the time. I only ever met Russians very occasionally, and then only in passing.

Senanga Secondary School had never had Russians on its staff before. News that two Russian teachers were definitely coming caused a buzz around the school compound for a while, but there was always so much to do getting ready for a new term, the fuss soon died down.

To be honest, their coming was a considerable nuisance to me. The school timetable was entirely my responsibility, in all its complexity. Fitting in all the classes was like playing a giant game of chess on a huge sheet of hardboard. A total of 3,600 different coloured golf-tee pegs, representing teachers, subjects and rooms, had to be slotted in to make each day a workable unit.

With the added complication of split subjects – girls to domestic science, boys to woodwork and so on – if you weren't careful you could end up with more classes than classrooms. It took me hours to rejig the board to accommodate the new arrivals.

There was no doubt that Galina Vasilyeva and her male colleague, Alex, were well qualified for the job, but although they were courteous and amiable, they didn't seem all that keen at first to mix socially. Ours was such a small community you couldn't help noticing.

I put their reserve down to language difficulties. Alex spoke fairly fluent English, but it wasn't hard to see that both of them had trouble tuning in to our various accents. Galina especially appeared to have problems understanding even the most simple conversations.

But they managed their classes well enough, and they gave us no cause to worry about their work.

*

2

The more I thought about it, the more Galina Vasilyeva's sudden pallor that afternoon bothered me. Had my voice been too loud? My tone a shade overbearing? Had my size, six feet plus and broad with it, intimidated her? Or had she simply misunderstood? She certainly kept out of my way as much as she could after that, and when we did meet, as we must, I got the disturbing impression that she was afraid of me.

I was away quite often on trips with my school chess team, playing in tournaments all over Zambia, and when I was around Senanga in the evenings most of my time was spent in the local bar with friends, downing a few beers and putting the world to rights.

I saw very little of Galina Vasilyeva outside school.

Frightened or not, though, she went on leaving stuff around the staffroom, and I often saw other members of staff reading it. Our African teachers seemed particularly interested, and once or twice I noticed them slipping some of the booklets into their pockets.

Finding myself alone in the staffroom during a free period one morning, I thought I'd better take a closer look at these 'absent-mindedly dropped' items.

They looked to me like nothing more than colourful glossy brochures praising the beautiful city of Moscow and inviting Zambians to make cultural and educational visits – hardly subversive.

There were photographs of the Kremlin with its famous golden domes, the Cathedral of St Basil, the Bolshoi Theatre, the Lenin State Library, the Moscow River ... The text was a bit repetitive, full of assurances about the warm welcome that was waiting for Zambian students at the Patrice Lumumba Friendship University ... 'peace and friendship'.

The writing style and the language were far too flowery for my taste, but the brochures seemed harmless enough. I was pretty naïve about international politics, then. By the time I began to understand the tactics of the Soviet game I was personally and inextricably involved.

Let me tell you our story, Galina's and mine.

3

1

England: 1968

Strange, isn't it, what one little twist of fate can lead to.

I was several months out of teacher training college and on my way to a job interview when a signals failure at Waterloo held up my train and changed the course of my life. This interview was for my first job as a qualified maths teacher, and I had high hopes of the outcome.

It was only a few months after the finish of my formal training as a mathematics teacher that I came across an advertisement in the *Times Educational Supplement* inviting qualified teachers to apply for a post in Kenya. This caught my interest at once.

The travel bug had bitten me early in life. In my boyhood, first in Lincolnshire and then in London, I roamed all over the place, sometimes alone and sometimes with friends.

When I was 13 the family moved to Peterborough, and I was ill for a long time after the move. Even when I was well again it took me quite a while to settle down there and start making new friends, but eventually I did, and began to enjoy life again. Living in a railway town gave me the chance to indulge my passion for steam trains, a pleasure that would stay with me all my life.

In my teens I discovered the Youth Hostels Association, and spent my school holidays cycling the length and breadth of Britain. Later, during college vacations, I hitchhiked across Western Europe equipped with only my college scarf and a haversack.

The idea of teaching abroad appealed to me very strongly. It excited my sense of adventure. Some of my friends had got involved with Voluntary Service Overseas, but I wasn't too keen on VSO work, mainly because there was so little money in it and I needed to be able to support myself.

The chance to go to Kenya was too good to miss. I got my application in straight away. I was invited to come up to London for an interview, but as luck would have it, a signals failure delayed my train outside Waterloo. By the time I got to the Ministry of Overseas Development (as the Overseas Development Administration was then known) the Kenya job had gone.

The ministry people were very sympathetic. 'Bad luck, old chap! There's something going in Zambia, though, any chance you might be interested in that?'

Kenya, Zambia, Timbuktu, it made no difference to me. All I wanted was an interesting post with a decent salary and a bit of a challenge about it.

The terms were pretty good. There was some kind of inducement allowance from the Ministry – as if I needed inducement to go to Africa! – and the Zambian Government would pay my local salary. I was to have a three-year contract, air tickets, and four days leave for every month worked. It sounded great to me.

In December 1968 I flew with British United Airways out of Heathrow Airport, bound for Lusaka, the capital city of Zambia. I was 25 years old and ready to step into a whole new world. Life was wonderful.

2

Zambia: 1968

My plane made a touchdown at Kampala in Uganda, then we flew on to Zambia and landed in the Copper Belt at Ndola. Ndola Airport still had international status at this time, and it was here I had my first encounter with the petty officialdom you have to learn to deal with all over Africa.

I got out my camera to take a souvenir photograph of the plane. From 50 yards away a uniformed policeman spotted me and came marching across the airfield. 'No photographing planes! It's not allowed!'

I had got on this plane at Heathrow in London, for heaven's sake! You could snap any kind of plane there any time you wanted. The plane was British, I was British, what was all the fuss about?

This stony-faced cop with his right hand on a holster was a far cry from your average British bobby. He gave me what sounded like a good ticking off, but my ear wasn't tuned to the local accent and most of the words went over my head.

Just as well, really. It wouldn't have done me any good at all if I'd punched him on the nose and got myself arrested the minute I set foot in Africa.

The moment my plane touched down at Lusaka International Airport and I saw the brand-new terminal building gleaming white in the afternoon sun, my spirits soared. Everything looked so clean, so fresh. A bright new omen for my bright new life.

From my first day in the capital I felt pretty much at home, because the administration was similar in so many ways to the UK. They drove on the left like us, and nearly everybody spoke English.

There were British people in Lusaka, in all spheres of work. This wasn't really surprising, as the country had only had full independence since 1964 and the Zambians were far from ready to do without our input.

Lusaka felt a lot more comfortable than countries I'd been to across the English Channel, where the people speak a different language and drive on the right. Many's the time I've had to run for my life trying to cross a road in Paris or Rome.

It took a while, though, to get used to the much slower way of doing things. Such a big change in the pace of life can make you feel frustrated and impatient, but after a while you learn to live with it. You have to. You soon realize it's pointless to get upset about having to wait an age for the smallest of services. The trick is to relax and accept things as they are.

The Lozi people of the Western Province are very friendly and polite. When I commented on this to a fellow expat he said, 'Yes, the locals have a joke that when a Lozi comes to town and walks down Cairo Road it takes him three days to get from one end to the other, because he has so many fellow visitors to greet. The people who live in the city abandoned these courtesies long ago. They're far too busy going about their business.'

Since the formal greeting involves a complicated ritual of bowing, then half-squatting and clapping, then bowing again: 'Mulumele sha' (Hello), 'Na zuh, ni lekula mina?' (I'm well, and you?'), it isn't hard to understand how much time it takes up.

I soon began to appreciate the benefits of Zambia's leisurely way of life. Nevertheless, it was comforting to know we were only a nine-hour flight from the UK, less time than it takes to drive from London to the North of Scotland. But it's a lot warmer in Africa.

*

8

My first contract was at Mankoya Secondary School. Mankoya was a bush station two hours' flight to the west and a touch north from Lusaka. The name 'Mankoya' was to be changed a year or two later to 'Kaoma' for some tribal reason or other, I was never quite sure what. I flew there soon after my few days' briefing in the capital.

When I stepped down from the plane on to the airstrip at Mankoya there seemed to be eyes staring at me from every direction. There wasn't a European in sight. It was like landing in one of those old Rider Haggard stories, *Allan Quatermain* or *King Solomon's Mines*, where the hero finds himself surrounded by spear-carrying natives intent on having him for lunch.

Of course, the people were actually taking very little notice of me. They were far too concerned with their own business to bother. But everything seemed so strange and so new to me, and my stomach was churning with apprehension. I was sweating so much in the unbelievable heat that my clothes were soaked through and sticking to my skin, and the clouds of dust I had to walk through got into my hair and my beard and clung to my wet clothing.

As if the hordes of flies that kept trying to settle on my face were not bad enough, I also had to keep swatting at a giant black wasp-like thing the size of a dragonfly. It was all very unpleasant.

Not an inch of the airport runway was tarred. My plane had landed on a flat stretch of dirt, and I could see nothing there but a tiny office and a one-roomed post office with postboxes attached to an outside wall.

So much for the long cold drink I'd been looking forward to. I was burning up with thirst.

All the locals were dressed in filthy-looking ragged clothing. The children had running noses and their shirts were so torn they hung in shreds around the poor skinny bodies. Pot bellies and bare bottoms stuck out of trousers that had seen better days. None of the children seemed to notice the flies that were crawling all over their faces. They didn't even bother to flick them away.

There were mothers with babies strapped to their backs, and women walking around with bundles wrapped in sheets balanced on their heads. I'd only ever seen this in pictures before. Nobody seemed the slightest bit worried about the dirty, under-fed, rabid-looking dogs that were roaming around quite freely.

The road to the school was nothing but a dirt track, and the only 'buildings' I passed were huts built of grass and mud, where women sat pounding maize while chickens pecked around their feet.

We were in the rainy season, yet there was hardly a sign of green anywhere. Everything was so dust-dry and grey, I could hardly believe what I was seeing. It was all so different, and such a depressing contrast to the lushness and colour I had been enjoying so much.

I had left tourist Africa far behind. This was true bush country, and I was beginning to realize what that meant.

What had I let myself in for? It was a very long way from Surrey to this primitive African outpost, where I seemed to be the only white man for miles.

I wasn't, of course. In next to no time I was settling into my first mixed bush secondary boarding school and getting to know my way around the long low buildings that were to be my home for at least the next year.

The teachers at Mankoya were nearly all British, but there were other nationalities here, too. We had a Zambian Head, Richard Lubasi, who was one of the first graduates from the University of Zambia, and an Irish priest, Father John, who taught Religious Education.

There were a few Canadians at Luampa Mission, but they were forty miles away down what can only be classed as a cart-track, so we seldom met. We did have visits from their doctor once every week or so, as we had no doctor on station at Kaoma, only nurses.

The deputy headmaster was a young man in his twenties, a conscientious and deeply religious person who commanded great respect in the village. His name was Peter, and it was he who explained what my duties would be and showed me around the school.

I was shocked at the bareness of the place. The paint on its walls was dingy, and nearly every classroom had broken windows with lethal-looking shards of glass sticking out of the frames. It reminded me of an army barracks without the fences.

But the worst thing of all was the dust that coated everything. There was hardly a blade of grass to be seen anywhere. This was what it meant to live with the Kalahari on your doorstep: dust, dust and more dust.

The schoolchildren wore a khaki-coloured uniform with short-sleeved jackets, reminding me of pictures I'd seen of peasants toiling in the paddy fields of China, all dressed alike in dingy grey. Our children seemed to blend into the dust like moving parts of the landscape.

Ours was only one of many new state secondary schools recently built throughout Zambia. At Mankoya, we offered a general education up to the Cambridge Overseas Certificate, an education good enough to take our students either to the University of Zambia or to a further education college. At the very least they would get a job in the civil service. Everybody was proud of the excellent record the school was building up.

It didn't take me long to realize how inadequately prepared I was for life in the bush.

My first trip to the shops in the village was something of a culture shock. There was hardly anything to buy but tins of fish and sacks of ground-up mealie meal. This was made from maize, and it was the people's staple food. They cooked it in pots and made it into a stiff dough and ate it with some kind of stewed fish or whatever vegetables happened to be available.

The small luxuries of life had gone. No milk, no bread, no marmalade, no bacon, no cornflakes, no potatoes ... and still two months of the term to go. What on earth was I going to live on?

Once a week an old Dakota flew up from Lusaka. You could hear the engine long before the plane materialized out of the heat haze. Every expatriate would be waiting at the airstrip to collect their post, hoping for word from back home. It didn't seem to matter that the news might be a month old. Maybe

11

there would be fresh meat on board for some lucky expat who could afford to buy it in Lusaka and have it ferried up.

Although the plane flew up regularly, I didn't have the money to fly back and forward to stock up my food supplies. For the foreseeable future I would have to depend on buying locally, and there was little enough to buy. Sometimes I bought bread, but all too often broke it open to find well-baked specimens of the insect life that swarmed and crawled around the bakehouse. I had a cook who sometimes made bread for me, from wheat flour if there was any available, or from maize if there wasn't.

The teaching staff lived in relative luxury, and we all had house boys or garden boys, sometimes both. These servants lived on the junior staff compound, as did the school clerical staff. They were housed in what was no better than a shanty town with outside water taps and lavatories.

Again and again, I asked myself what on earth I was doing in such a place. This was a far cry from the macho bachelor expat life I had come to Africa for. Mankoya offered nothing remotely like the comfortable, sociable and jolly times I had enjoyed with my friends in London and which I had confidently expected to carry on in Zambia.

Life took a turn for the brighter, though, on the day I saw the beer lorry trundle up to the local bar, hauling its loaded trailer. According to folklore, the beer lorry gets through no matter what, even if the road is cut off.

In spite of my doubts I got by, and soon had my usual high spirits back. This was mainly due to the deputy head, Peter, who kindly let me stay in his house for a few days and fed me till I was better able to fend for myself. He wasn't much older than me, but he looked after me like a surrogate father, and I'll always be grateful for that.

It was Peter, too, who explained the local customs and traditions, so I would know what and what not to do.

'*Never* call anyone stupid,' he told me. 'Not even in a joking way. It's the most dreadful insult.'

And on no account was it acceptable to call anyone 'boy',

Peter said. 'This is a word indelibly and for ever associated with South Africa and its racist apartheid regime. The freedom of the people there is sorely oppressed. To call a man "boy" is to stab him with a weapon of contempt.'

My very colonial-looking hat from Tropicadilly in London was soon put away as unsuitable wear for a newly independent nation. It was much better to adopt the usual civil servant uniform of short-sleeved shirt, shorts and long socks.

In those early days, mindful of stories and films about scorpions and spiders and snakes, I was meticulous about tapping the heels of my shoes at least twice before putting them on. It was also prudent to peer carefully into the lavatory, in case a snake might have curled itself around the lip of the bowl.

I knew very little about snakes, but there were plenty of tales going round about certain kinds of cobra which people swore could spit venom over two and a half metres. I was not prepared to take chances with safety. And like a good European, I religiously took my Cloraquin malaria tables on schedule.

I had been in Mankoya just over a year when one of our pupils died, a boy called Mwitumwa, not quite 16 years old.

Mwitumwa's home was about 200 miles from Mankoya, a two-day trek through bush country without even a dirt road. We had no ice or any other means of preserving his body. He would have to be buried within a few hours.

We made every effort to reach his parents. We sent a driver in a Land Rover, the only vehicle that could cope with the rough terrain, but we knew it was hopeless. Mwitumwa's people could never get to Mankoya in time for his funeral.

You only begin to understand what it means to live in such a close community when you see the school prefects making a coffin in the woodwork department and watch a dead boy's friends working together to dig his grave. The sound of those children wailing in their grief will stay with me for the rest of my days.

We were in the process of changing headmasters at this time, and both John Whittingham, the incoming head, and the outgoing head, Richard Lubasi, helped the school captain and his deputy to carry the coffin the short distance to the local burial ground close to the school.

There were no boundary fences, and I felt almost as if we were burying Mwitumwa in the school grounds. I had never before known such a sense of community. For the first time, I felt at one with my African friends.

I began to get involved in providing out-of-class entertainment for the pupils, something that was to provide me with much pleasure and satisfaction throughout my years in Zambia.

Here in Mankoya we showed films on Saturday nights, using an antiquated Bell and Howell projector. It soon became one of my many jobs to bring back a selection of films from the film library in Lusaka every time I had a chance to go to the capital.

None of these children had seen films before, so their reactions were quite a contrast to the sophisticated attitude of the children I had taught in the UK.

Their innocence was touching. I'll never forget the evening they tried to rescue Tarzan by shouting and throwing stones at a snake that was attacking him. Our 'screen' was a whitewashed rectangle of wall, so no damage was done. The stones simply bounced off. But Tarzan strangled the snake, and there was much clapping and cheering. The children were convinced they had helped.

Another time, we showed a film in which a couple were seen kissing in the back seat of a car. As the pair slid down out of view, the entire school stood up to see what was going on.

I had a lot of fun helping to put on plays and quizzes, too. We wanted to make these Saturday nights a complete relaxation from school work. I was delighted when some of the pupils got interested in chess, which was one of my hobbies.

The enjoyment I found in these activities helped me to keep a sense of proportion when I got fed up with all the tiresome local difficulties like water shortages and lousy food.

*

14

I kept my spirits up by planning where to go and what to do in my holidays. As an unattached young Britisher, I regarded the whole of Africa as my playground.

The friends I had made during my short stay in Lusaka were mostly young bachelors like myself. Many of them were teachers too, so our leaves often coincided. We soon established a network of contacts, organized so we could keep in touch through notes pinned to notice boards in selected hotels in the capitals we passed through on our travels.

In Lusaka, we used the Lusaka Hotel on Cairo Road, right in the centre of town. In Dar-es-Salaam, it was the Africa Hotel, in Nairobi the Stanley Hotel. 'Peter Young was here July 5th – back August 1st . . .' and so on. We were keen to enjoy life to the full, and Africa had plenty to offer.

I couldn't afford a vehicle of my own at first, so had to travel on local transport or hitch a ride to get around. I always found bus trips exhilarating, and sometimes they could be scary, especially if the bus got bogged down in a swamp in tsetse-fly country. Those little beggars can't half bite, and there's always a risk of sleeping sickness.

But the best way of all to travel the country was in a four-wheel-drive vehicle, teaming up with whoever wanted to come along. The thrill of shooting off in a Land Rover never palled. Off we would go across the Kalahari or over to Kafue Game Park or deep into bush country. We got to see places where no tourist had ever set foot. These adventures were what had attracted most of us to Africa in the first place.

Memories of journeys past and dreams of journeys to come kept me going during those lonely months deep in the African bush.

After just over three years in Mankoya, which was now known by its new name of Kaoma, I was offered promotion to housemaster in Mongu, the administrative capital of Western Province. Mongu lies 110 miles west of Kaoma, and is much bigger, more like a small town.

The township sits on a hill high enough to clear the waterline when the rainy season comes and the Zambezi floods the plain below for miles around. I could never understand why local people went on building huts on the flood plain year after year, only to see them break up and float away on the rising floodwater that inevitably came with the rains.

Mongu has a ramshackle little harbour, which struck me as a bit of an oddity, as the Zambezi is five or six miles away and only linked to Mongu by a narrow canal.

The harbour lies down a hill from the Liambai Hotel. 'Liambai' is the Lozi name for the Zambezi River. In the evenings we used to sit on the hotel terrace and watch the local fishermen paddling in and out of the harbour. They would tie up and stand in their canoes, offering freshly caught fish for trade.

There were some people selling fruit, and some offering live chickens which flapped about in little baskets made from twigs tied together with tree bark. Most evenings, the whole harbour area became a floating market-place.

It was all very picturesque, especially when the setting sun bathed the scene in a golden glow, turning the boats and the fishermen into floating silhouettes.

In my new job I was also careers master, and this gave me a chance to develop the boys' interest in chess. Before very long I had become Zambia Schools chairman and was involved in organizing tournaments in Lusaka, with schools attending from all over the country.

It was a full life, and a good one. What more could I possibly want?

3

Senanga, Zambia: 1975

I worked my second contract in Mongu, and began my third contract there at the beginning of 1975, but only a few weeks later I was transferred to Senanga Secondary School, some 55 miles to the south.

I was sad to leave Mongu. My three years there had been very happy, and I had made a lot of friends. But I wasn't moving very far away, so that was some consolation.

The road connecting Senanga to Mongu was a nightmare of ruts and potholes sometimes a couple of feet deep, but I had my own car now, a Datsun 120Y, and thought little of such a short journey.

I've always loved driving. My father let me learn on his Austin 7 in a railway yard when I was only 10, so although some of the roads in Africa were pretty rough, I always managed to get to where I wanted to go.

Senanga sits on the banks of the Zambezi, well above the flood plain. The point where the road touched the school was only 100 yards or so from the river, and my house was only another 150 yards farther away.

The river looks calm and inviting here, but it has a very fast flow past Senanga. This was a minor danger, however, compared to the hippos and crocodiles. Only a few miles from Senanga the road to Sesheke and Livingstone crossed the river at a place called Kazangoola, 'the place of crocodiles'. Nobody swam in the Zambezi at Senanga if they had any sense.

One local teacher from Senanga Primary School was eaten

by a crocodile not long after I got there. We had a collection for her in the Secondary School. She was the only person I heard of being killed by a crocodile. Hippos were far more dangerous.

The fishing was supposed to be wonderful, though, and I was looking forward to trying my hand at catching tiger-fish, something I'd often heard my friends in Mongu boasting about.

Senanga was not the most peaceful place to be living in at this time, and access to the area was restricted, the only foreigners allowed to come and go freely being those of us employed by the Zambian government.

Our school was situated uncomfortably close to the road used by Dr Savimbi's UNITA freedom fighters as they travelled up and down the country. We didn't enjoy being jolted awake in the middle of the night by bombs blasting around us, as happened all too frequently.

UNITA stands for 'National Union for Total Independence of Angola', and at this time President Kenneth Kaunda's Zambian government was enthusiastic in its support for their fight.

We had some of Dr Savimbi's relatives as pupils, and we often saw him in our local bar. He looked about 40, but it was hard to tell exactly because of his beard.

Jonas Savimbi always came across as a pleasant sort of man, and he never failed to send a round of drinks over to the expat teachers, with a smile and a wave. We knew this was purely a public-relations exercise, but it was very well done just the same.

The UNITA freedom fighters were a well-disciplined bunch, far better behaved than the Zambian army. It was common gossip that the Zambian soldiers camped as close as they could get to the school because they were afraid of the bombs. They didn't think anybody would deliberately bomb schoolchildren.

These Zambians were an unruly mob. They used to throw tins of corned beef over the perimeter fence near the dormitories to try to get to know our secondary-school girls. We kept a close watch on our pupils, especially at night, and I never heard of any actual physical contact between pupils and soldiers.

18

It wasn't a lot of fun having this rabble around, but it was a lot worse for the Lozi people, whose farms and villages were regularly ravaged in the fighting. The people living in remote regions far from even the dirt roads were terrified of the freedom fighters and the South African bombing. They were too scared of being attacked to go out on to the fields, so no crops were planted and the people went hungry. The nuns and missionaries did what they could to feed the people, but food was scarce and travel could be difficult and dangerous.

And as if all this wasn't enough, the expat grapevine was red-hot with rumours about the Soviets. Some of the Russians coming into Zambia now, we heard, were military advisers passing themselves off as civilians. Some of my colleagues were getting quite steamed up about 'Reds under the bed'.

I preferred to sit on the terrace with a cool beer and watch the fishermen in their boats on the river, the rhino coming down to the water to drink, and the colonies of bright-plumed weaver birds flying in and out of their extraordinary hanging nests.

As it turned out, the rumours about Russian teachers coming were true. They arrived in September.

4

___

Moscow: August 1974–September 1975

For Galina, it began with a summons over the intercom in the school where she taught mathematics. 'Galina Vasilyeva – please come to my office after the lesson.'

The call was nothing out of the ordinary. Galina was on very friendly terms with Lydia Ivanovna, who had been her headmistress for several years now.

'You promised to go shopping with me today, you remember, Galina?'

'Yes, of course.'

'There's something I have to do first. I must finish this report, then you won't mind if we go past the Ministry so I can hand it in?'

The report Lydia Ivanovna was working on was for the Ministry of Education. She was filling in details about the number of teachers in the school and their pupils' examination results.

She turned the document round and indicated a particular question. 'Read that – Question 15A.' Question 15A asked if there was anyone on the school staff who could be recommended for promotion or for sending abroad.

Galina was mystified. Why was her headmistress showing her this question?

For teachers in the Soviet Union, 'going abroad' was something that simply didn't happen. There was plenty of speculation that maybe a few people from the Foreign Office were allowed to go on diplomatic trips, but nobody ever seemed to know for sure. This had to be something special.

Galina sometimes saw foreign tourists getting out of their special buses around the Kremlin or in Gorky Street, but she never went near them. Talking to foreigners was forbidden. Everybody knew there were watchers everywhere ready to report any Muscovite who spoke to a tourist, and nobody wanted to risk their career.

Like all her generation, Galina had been taught from childhood that foreigners only came to mock and to criticize. Hers was the best country in the world, and those who were not lucky enough to live here wanted only to destroy it.

Foreigners were like beings from another planet. It was safer to steer clear of them. Galina had been teaching for 13 years, and was proud of her successful career. She preferred to play safe. But she was young and full of energy, and for a long time now she had been longing for something exciting to happen.

Now, here was Lydia Ivanovna holding out this document and asking, 'Do you want to go abroad?'

Trying not to show her excitement, Galina said, 'I wouldn't mind.'

'If you want, put your name down on the form.'

If you want . . . Oh yes, she wanted. Very much, she wanted.

She walked with Lydia Ivanovna to the Ministry of Education of the Russian Republic to give in the report. Then they went shopping.

Galina knew Lydia Ivanovna had never been abroad herself but had been for many years an elected member of the Soviet of People's Deputies, serving on a local district council where one of her responsibilities was the allocation of telephone numbers. There were very few telephone lines available, and you needed a very special reason to get access to one, otherwise you were on a waiting list for up to 10 years.

If you could offer special currency roubles, however, Lydia Ivanovna was the person who could speed things up and get you connected in weeks, even without a special reason. This kind of trade-off was rife throughout the Soviet Union, in every area, at every level. Everybody knew about it, everybody accepted it.

Currency roubles were only issued to people like Lydia Ivanovna who held special positions in the government, to selected members of the armed services, and to anyone lucky enough to earn foreign currency abroad.

It was a criminal offence for Soviet citizens to hold foreign currency, so if you earned money abroad you had to deposit every penny you didn't need for living expenses in a special bank in Moscow. The State was desperate for foreign currency, so the dollars or pounds you deposited there were converted to currency roubles, each worth eight times the value of an ordinary rouble. You got your currency roubles in the form of vouchers called *valuta* certificates, and these could only be held by Soviet citizens.

It was a typically complicated kind of system. There were many different kinds of currency roubles, and each kind had to be spent in specified shops. For instance, you couldn't walk into the armed services currency shop unless you had armed services currency roubles; you couldn't shop in government shops unless, like Lydia Ivanovna, you had government currency roubles.

The currency shops were called *Beryozka* shops. Most were on the outskirts of Moscow, hidden away from those who had no access to them and so unobtrusive you could walk past them if you didn't know they were there.

There was always a man at the door ready to keep you out unless you could prove your right to be there, and that right depended entirely on being able to produce the correct currency roubles. If the guard happened to be absent and outsiders wandered in and tried to buy something, they would be thrown out by specially trained bouncers.

For those lucky enough to have the correct roubles, these shops were like Aladdin's cave. Here you could find almost anything you ever dreamed of. Clothes, shoes, cosmetics, jewellery, soft furnishings, wallpaper, even handles for your doors. Everything you could possibly want was there, at incredibly low prices, in lavish quantity, and with plenty of choice.

There were *Beryozka* shops inside the international hotels, too, where tourists could spend their own currency. These were stocked with the best of Russian products like caviar, furs and Russian curios, as well as luxury imports. Ordinary Russians were never allowed anywhere near these shops.

Lydia Ivanovna did nearly all her shopping in *Beryozka* shops. Here she spent the currency roubles she was paid by people keen to show their gratitude in return for telephone allocations.

She said she enjoyed Galina's company and trusted her taste, and Galina was always happy to go along, even though she had no currency roubles of her own and could only look, touch and smell the delicious 'forbidden fruits'.

As she caressed luscious silk scarves from France, featherlight knitwear from Italy, soft leather shoes from Spain, she dreamed of having her own currency roubles. To be able to buy such things for herself – how wonderful that would be.

Galina didn't really envy her friend – well, not very much. Lydia Ivanovna was very good to her, and helped her in many ways. The older woman, in her fifties, treated Galina like a daughter. She had even helped her find a bedsit in the centre of Moscow, not far from the school.

This was only a small flat, but for the first time in her life Galina had privacy, a great luxury in Moscow, where several families usually had to share a communal flat. The State allocated one room to each family, and everyone who lived in the flat shared the same kitchen, bathroom and toilet.

Galina's mother was a university graduate who worked all her adult life as a chemical engineer in extremely hazardous conditions, but she had never had the privacy Galina enjoyed now. Galina owed her comparative comfort entirely to her friend's patronage.

Finding furniture was just one of the difficulties Muscovites had to cope with. You had to put your name on a waiting list, and the wait could be anything up to three years. You were given a number in the queue, and every month you had to re-register your intent to buy, in the open air and waiting for hours, even in sub-zero temperatures. If you failed to do this you went right back to the end of the queue.

Even when your turn came up, you could only buy whatever happened to be available that day. You had no choice of style or colour, or even of size. Bad luck if there was nothing to fit your room. The dreary procedure was the same for buying wallpaper, carpets, material to make curtains . . .

Thanks to Lydia Ivanovna, Galina was able to bypass the queues, and soon had her flat comfortably furnished with a good carpet and beautiful Yugoslav furniture. She had a mahogany wall unit, and a settee and chairs upholstered in dark green. In Moscow, such luxury didn't seem real.

So Galina was living pretty well. She had interesting work, an influential patroness, and a few close friends she treasured.

But what a chance she had been offered, so suddenly, so unexpectedly. She had seldom been out of Moscow, only to summer camps when she was a child and for an occasional holiday by the Black Sea. She had been on educational trips to Romania and to Bulgaria, but always inside Communist borders and always closely supervized.

Now, here was a chance to go abroad, to see Africa, to see the world beyond the Republic and its satellites. Here was a chance to have her own currency roubles. How could she not take it?

'Of course, you'll have to join the Party,' Lydia Ivanovna told her. This was no surprise. It was inconceivable for someone who was not a Party member to be trusted with an overseas posting.

Although she had nothing against the Party, Galina had never made any effort to join, mainly because membership would take up too much of her free time.

You were given tasks to do, and of course you were obliged to do them. You were expected to persuade people to subscribe to *Pravda*, to spread ideas to non-Party people, to help with housing problems and, of course, to report cases of wrong

24

behaviour. You were also required to attend regular meetings, where Party officials interrogated you about your life, your views and your ideals.

On top of this, you had to learn by heart pages and pages of the Manifesto of the Communist Party, all of Lenin's speeches, and all the political history of the Soviet Union. And, as if all this was not enough, you were also supposed to make a close study of Karl Marx's *Das Kapital*.

Membership cost money, too. The Party demanded a large contribution from your salary, and no argument. And before you could join at all, you had to find three high-ranking Party members to recommend you. It seemed like altogether too much hassle.

But now Galina wrote her application: 'Please accept me as a member of the Communist Party because ... I want to be in the avant-garde of the building of Communism in the Soviet Union and the whole world, and I want to show examples to non-Communists ... in my work, in my morals, in everything.'

She swore a solemn oath that in every respect she would be a shining model of Russian citizenship and teaching.

Galina Vasilyeva had little idea what was happening in the rest of her country, let alone the rest of the world. Anything bad that was said about Russia was condemned through the State-controlled media as anti-Soviet propaganda from the West. She knew nothing about the Gulag till she was outside the Soviet Union.

Like all Soviet schoolchildren, she was taught to worship each leader in turn. When a new leader denounced his predecessor, the children got a little confused, but no one ever doubted the system. It was the best in the world, and Communism was the future.

Galina remembered clearly the day her teacher came into the classroom and told all the children to cross out every page in their history textbook that made any reference to Stalin. Even this did not shake the children's idealistic belief in the State. They were only relieved at not having to sit the history exam that year.

25

The children of the Soviet Union were brought up to believe that their country had a special mission in the world. In the West, everybody lived for themselves, but in Russia people lived for the great ideals of Communism, of Lenin, of Marx. Your personal being was secondary to spirit and country, and patriotism was always to be the most important thing in your life.

The history the children learned in school taught that the West was always trying to destroy this new experiment, this ideal of equality, and had been trying to destroy it from the earliest days of the Revolution. They should never forget all the sacrifices made over the years, all the people who died trying to build this beautiful future.

The West didn't want Russia to change history and lead the whole world to Communism. But the Russians were right, they had the right message, they were like Messiahs, so there was nothing else to say.

The children were taught to worship their leaders, to look up to them and revere them like royalty. It was a sad irony that Communism, the doctrine that condemned religion, had almost become a religion itself.

So Galina applied for Party membership. She learned all the right answers, she knew what had to be said, and said it. She went through all the motions, managed every stage, every interview, but it meant absolutely nothing to her.

Going through the motions didn't make her a better person, nor did it make her a worse one. It was simply a means to an end. As far as she knew, it didn't mean much to anybody else, either.

Like everyone she knew, Galina led a double life. At work she conformed to the system and behaved with circumspection and decorum. But evenings and weekends were different. She could relax with friends, and feel as free as they did to tell political anecdotes, make political jokes, and criticize the bureaucratic attitudes of some official or another.

Galina moved in a sophisticated circle, part of Moscow's intelligentsia. Her friends were lecturers, teachers, journalists, lawyers, television artists . . . all university-educated, all sharing the same kind of subtle, witty, sharp-edged humour.

The political jokes these people enjoyed would have gone over the heads of most of the population. In Russia, you belonged to either the educated classes or the lower classes. There was nothing in between.

The difference between the city and the country in Britain is little more than a change of location, but in Russia to go to the country is to drop back a century in time to log cabins, no running water and no sanitation.

Galina and her friends had no qualms about questioning the way things were run and making jokes at the expense of bureaucratic anomalies and self-seeking officials. They regarded this as their right. But they could not accept criticism from the West.

She believed absolutely that there can't be anything wrong with the idea of all people being equal. The problems were not caused by the system itself but by the people in power, who were allowing the system to run down. These people were corrupt. Almost without exception they abused their positions, and this process of corruption filtered down through every level, right down to the peasant in the field.

Corruption permeated society. You could do nothing about it, so you learned to live with it, adapt to it, and use it. It was futile and dangerous to challenge things openly. You had to learn how to make the system work for you, not against you.

When Galina confided to her closest friends that she was joining the Party so she could go abroad, everyone accepted her reasons as perfectly valid.

Her friend L was delighted. 'That's marvellous,' he said. 'I'm hoping to go myself. So is Alex.'

This was welcome news to Galina. She knew L's wife, and it would be good to talk about her plans with someone she could trust.

So the preparations went on. Galina had to get signed documents from the psychiatric centre to prove she was not a psychiatric patient and never had been. She had to get signed proof from the venereal diseases clinic that she was not suffering from any sexually related diseases and never had been. Heart and lungs, bones and blood, nervous system, eyes, teeth ... every detail was checked and double-checked. The Ministry must surely be deeply concerned about her health.

She didn't learn the true reason till very much later, when a colleague told her that the health checks were thorough because the Soviets didn't want their citizens incurring large medical bills the State would have to pay out of currency reserves.

It took nearly two months, but eventually her certificate of fitness came through. The whole tedious process would be repeated the following year, when Galina had completed her English Language course.

There were other special procedures, too, a seemingly endless series of interviews. You had to be approved by three Big Brothers: the Party, the Trade Unions, and the Administration.

All three praised Galina for her highly professional attributes and assessed her as 'politically trustworthy and morally stable'. She could safely be recommended for a teaching post in Africa, where she would represent the Soviet Union as a true friend of the African.

Three signatures and a rubber stamp. Another hurdle cleared. But the process wasn't finished even yet. Before Galina could be seconded for the required English Language course, back she had to go to her school for a character reference, then to the Party Committee of her District, then to the Moscow City and Central Committee for yet more signatures and more rubber stamps.

Galina learned English by a very unorthodox method devised by a professor of psychology at Sofia in Bulgaria, Professor Lozanoff. This professor had travelled the world with his method, and the results were reported to be excellent.

Six or seven students sat informally in chairs and a teacher gave them roles to play in a continuing story, rather like a soap opera. Galina was Linda, a singer, and as she could never sing to save her life she had to put up with a good deal of teasing.

Two or three of the students had already studied English at school and at university, so they started with a considerable advantage. The only language Galina had studied was German, so she was delighted to find her hard work soon put her on a more or less even footing with everyone else.

She didn't learn vocabulary or grammar. She learned the meaning of the text sentence by sentence, through a combination of repetition and role-playing. The theory was that if the students were immersed in the language they couldn't fail to learn it.

Soon the class was doing mathematics in English, politics in English, and reading English language newspapers like the *Morning Star* and the *Moscow News*. By the end of the 10-month course Galina felt confident she had mastered the English language at least as much as she needed to.

Even in the language class, selection was still going on. The best candidates were selected for Zambia. Galina was one of the best. She would go to Zambia.

5

Zambia: September 1975

As there were no direct flights from Moscow to Zambia, Galina's party had to travel via Tanzania and make a two-day stopover in Dar-es-Salaam. When Galina stepped down from the plane at Dar-es-Salaam airport, she felt the African heat like a physical force.

The teachers had been warned their arrival in September was bad timing as far as the climate was concerned. It would soon be October, the 'suicide month', when the temperature would soar and the air grow torpid and heavy with approaching rain.

A representative from the Russian Embassy was waiting to meet the party, and the newcomers were glad to have help, even L, who was usually so self-confident. Very few of them had travelled outside the Communist bloc before, and never without an escort.

They were quite a large group, about 20 people, and they were told to stay together. None of them knew anything about passport control or how to fill in the routine forms on arrival. They were completely dependent on their more experienced leaders. And their leaders took care not to mention duty-free entitlements.

Months later, Galina would discover that the whole party's duty-free allowances of alcohol and tobacco had been collected behind their backs and taken to the Embassy. Their minders took their tickets and passports, and helped themselves to everything they could get their hands on. This was how the select party of teachers was 'looked after'.

The man from the Embassy took them to a hotel, where they were relieved to find effective air-conditioning. The Embassy would be looking after them during their stopover, they were told.

Galina didn't have the slightest notion anyone was watching her. She believed only that her welfare was being safeguarded.

Over the next two days Galina's main concern was to keep out of the heat as much as possible, so she saw very little of Dar-es-Salaam. None of the party were allowed to explore the town without an escort. She spent most of her time with Alex and L and L's wife, a pretty woman who was obviously enjoying all the attention the Russians were attracting.

Galina tried to cheer up Alex, who was upset because his wife had backed out of the trip as soon as she learned they would not be living in 'civilized' Lusaka, but in a remote bush township.

At the end of the stopover the four friends were separated from the rest of the party and flown on to Lusaka.

Even in Lusaka, the capital of the country in which they were to live and work, the Russian teachers were allowed no liberty. They were ordered not to leave the Embassy compound. Embassy officials confiscated their passports 'for safe keeping'. There were Western spies all over the place, they were warned, who were desperate to get hold of Russian passports because they wanted names and addresses 'for their foul purposes'.

Knowing no better, Galina didn't question this. Everybody knew, didn't they, that Western embassies were not at all interested in looking after their people. The teachers should feel grateful to their own Embassy for taking such good care of them. Russians always looked after Russians.

And even if they didn't like this confinement, they knew better than to complain. They were in Zambia on two-year contracts, and they would only be given a further assignment abroad if they behaved themselves and obeyed orders. If they were not 'good', if they gave the slightest sign of stepping out of line, they would never be allowed out of the USSR again.

*

Russians who came to Africa each had their own reasons. Most wanted a car, an impossible dream for people at home. Families came to Africa primarily to buy cars and to earn currency roubles. They seldom came for any altruistic reason, contrary to what the Africans were led to believe.

Galina had no particular feelings about teaching in Africa. White, brown or black, the pupils were all the same to her. Like everyone she knew, like Alex, like L, she wanted to achieve status, to pull herself up to a higher level. She didn't want a car, but there were plenty of other things she did want, the kind of luxurious goods she lusted after every time she went with Lydia Ivanovna to the *Beryozka* shops.

Their salaries were paid in pounds into bank accounts in Moscow, but the Russian teachers were not allowed to spend pounds in Russia. They could draw money in local currency for living expenses in Africa, but in Russia they could only draw this money as currency roubles.

Galina had been given 40 kwachas in Zambian currency to tide her over till her first salary came through. This was worth about £20 at that time.

She knew from what friends had told her that no Russians ever bought clothing or shoes in Zambia. They brought pasta and dried soups in their luggage, and relied on parcels coming from parents and friends in the USSR. Galina had heard reports of people fainting from hunger because they wouldn't spend any money, even on food. They tried to live on the absolute minimum. Every possible penny went into that precious account in Moscow.

In Lusaka the small party of four stayed in the Embassy compound, where the Embassy people kept a very close eye on them. On the day Galina and Alex were to move on to Senanga, a VIP with the title of Chairman of the Trade Delegation came to talk to them. L whispered in Galina's ear, 'You know he's a colonel in the KGB, don't you?'

Galina hadn't known. She wondered why L was telling her this. Everybody knew L's parents had connections with the KGB, but if he worked for them himself, he kept very quiet about it. She was still puzzling over this comment when the VIP began to speak. Every word the man uttered was an instruction of some kind. Instruction followed instruction. It was like listening to a recording of the Party Manifesto.

With their ears still ringing, Galina and Alex got ready to be driven out to the airport to catch a plane to their school in Senanga. L and his wife were staying on in the capital, where L would be taking up his new job.

As they said good-bye Alex joked, 'Come and visit us soon if they ever let you out of here.'

6

Senanga, Zambia: September–December 1975

In Senanga, Alex had to share a house, but because Galina was the only single woman teacher in the school she was given a whole house to herself. It was a good house, with a kitchen, a bathroom, three bedrooms and an open-plan sitting room. The doors to all the other rooms opened off the sitting room. She learned later it was built in the English 'bungalow' style.

She had never had so much space to herself before. She should have been ecstatic. Unfortunately, she had nothing with her but a couple of pieces of hand luggage. The plane was overloaded, and Galina's luggage was among the excess baggage that had to be taken off again and left behind. It should have come on the next plane, but there was still no sign of it.

The Embassy in Lusaka had promised to arrange for all the luggage to be forwarded to Dar-es-Salaam, where it would be taken care of and sent on, but nobody bothered to check and, as far as Galina could tell, the whole lot was still at the airport in Moscow.

So Galina found herself living in a spacious house where she should have been comfortable, but with no cleaning equipment, no cooking utensils, no food and no money. All her crockery and cutlery, her pasta and salami, her clothes and her bed-linen were still in Moscow. So too, she guessed, was her salary.

She couldn't understand why neither her personal possessions nor her money were coming through, when there seemed to be no problem with deliveries of the brochures she

34

was supposed to distribute in the school. Two parcels of this literature arrived in Senanga the day after she did.

To cap everything, the town water pump and the school generator were both out of action, and she had neither water nor electricity. The inch of water in the bottom of the ancient water tank that served her house was coated with green slime. It was impossible to use without boiling.

There were two stoves in the kitchen, one so black it must be meant for burning wood, the other a much smaller one for paraffin, but there was no fuel for either. Where was she supposed to get paraffin, a saucepan, a cup, a spoon . . .? As for going out to gather wood . . . what kind of impression would that give the local children who might soon be her pupils?

The entire township lay under a thick blanket of fine grey sand, inches deep so the shortest walk left you filthy. Keeping clean was a problem for everyone. For Galina, it was a nightmare.

She was starving, she felt grubby, and in the unrelenting heat she had a constant raging thirst. She had never been in such a situation in her life before, not even as a child just after the Second World War. Then, she had known deprivation and discomfort, cold and hunger. Then, there were vermin. One of her earliest memories was of waking to find a rat climbing on to her bed.

Now there was no war, yet here she was without food, without clean water, without a change of clothing, without money. Now there were insects. Cockroaches, flies, mosquitoes, ants . . . Was this how her Embassy was taking care of her?

Galina presented herself as decently as she could at the school, 50 yards' walk from her house. She thought the brick-built school didn't look too bad, given its remote situation. The Zambian teachers and pupils looked happy enough and reasonably well turned-out, she was pleased to see.

Outside the school, however, she found things very different. Here she saw poverty that made her own problems fade into insignificance. A lack of adequate feeding was all too evident in the people's pot bellies and rotten teeth. Even the youngest children bore visible signs of malnutrition in their distended bellies and skinny spindly legs. Skeletal dogs skulked around the township. Even the cows seemed little more than rickles of bones under loose covers of dusty hide.

She wondered how long it would be till she could start eating again.

Without realizing it, Alex came to Galina's rescue a couple of days later, with an invitation on behalf of his Scottish housemaster, Steve Jones. At Steve's house they drank tea and ate biscuits, and she had never tasted anything so good in her life.

Alex had found a small store that sold paraffin, and Galina dipped into her tiny hoard of kwachas to buy just enough to fuel her paraffin stove. The water supply had been restored, but everyone warned her not to drink the water without first boiling it thoroughly. Having seen the sludge in the water tank and the yellow-brown syrup that trickled out of the tap in her kitchen, she would have done so even without this advice.

A shake-out of her hand luggage yielded a packet of dried vegetable soup. She made it last two days.

News that Russian teachers were coming had apparently caused great excitement among the school staff. This was quite an event, it seemed. A few days after Alex and Galina arrived, one of the British women teachers, Myra Harrison, invited them both to dinner. Myra was Head of the English Department.

Other members of the teaching staff came along to Myra's house later in the evening, all very curious about Russia and asking many questions. The problem was that although they all spoke English, they had such a mixture of accents Galina could hardly believe they were all talking the same language. Nobody had told her about regional accents. English was English.

She had learned the language in Moscow from a Muscovite who spoke with the same accent as she did. She was completely thrown by a Liverpool or a Geordie or a Midlands accent. As for the Scottish accent – well, forget it.

Luckily their hostess, being a teacher of English, spoke with almost no accent, and Galina was very relieved to find she could understand quite easily everything Myra said.

Kind and welcoming though everyone was, she couldn't help feeling strange and isolated. She stayed as close to Alex as she could, and she was glad when the evening was over.

Faces, names, voices ... everything swirled around in her brain. She did recall clearly, though, one man who made his presence felt throughout the evening. This was the very large, very loud Englishman who had taken her round the school on her first day. His name, she remembered, was Peter Young.

There was a sizeable mixed community living in the school compound: African, English, Indian and Pakistani. Their numbers were frequently swelled by people travelling through Zambia who enjoyed a stopover in the convivial company of the staff of Senanga Secondary School. Galina had never met so many nationalities. Their talk made her head swim.

The Zambians, too, had an accent which made their English difficult for her to understand, especially some of the locals, who spoke a kind of pidgin English.

She carried a small Russian-English language dictionary with her wherever she went, and this became something of a joke.

The school sent a Zambian painter to do up her house, a good man, very religious, called Kauawa. Galina wanted to discuss colour schemes with him, but with every other word she had to say, 'Wait, wait, wait,' while she flicked through the pages of her dictionary. One day Kauawa asked, quite seriously, 'Madam, is that your Holy Bible?'

Alex got along better, as he was much more relaxed with the English language. He had been abroad before and had had the opportunity to use it. He talked with everybody.

Now there were no Russian officials around, Alex began to disregard his orders not to mix socially. A gregarious man, he missed his wife very badly and said he needed the company. He knew he could trust Galina not to report him. Soon he was doing his best to persuade her to come with him to the bar so they could both join in the card games that went on nearly every night.

37

Galina could never relax in this bar. Everything about the place made her head ache, the gaudily painted bright blue walls, the flashy bar-girls who were always available to entertain the local men, and the never-ending beat of loud African music.

Loud as the noise was, though, she soon came to recognise a laugh that was even louder, a roar that positively boomed around the bar. She always knew when the big Englishman was there.

Although everybody was friendly and welcoming, Galina never really felt part of the company, certainly not in the way Alex did. She felt too inhibited to talk to people because she could never be sure she would understand what they said in reply.

With maths, though, it was different. This was her field. She loved maths, and felt completely at home with the subject. She was delighted and gratified to find her pupils applauding at the end of the lesson and saying, 'Don't go,' they enjoyed it so much.

Apart from her lessons, Galina's life in Senanga for the next three months was a test of endurance.

She was even more distressed when she lost Alex's company after only a few weeks. He was very lonely, he said, without his wife and family, and to add to his troubles he was suffering from a chronic arthritic condition in his feet. He was finding it increasingly painful to trudge through the deep sand that clogged every road in the township.

He decided he couldn't bear the loneliness and the constant pain, and requested permission to go home. He left at the end of October.

With Alex gone, Galina felt more alone than ever. The nearest Russians were 55 miles away in Mongu. She had no transport, and still had no money. Parcels of brochures arrived regularly, but no salary. She was getting no answer, either, to her appeals for her luggage to be found. Had it not been for some of her fellow teachers' hospitality, she might have starved.

The Indian and Pakistani teachers in particular were

delighted to open their doors to a new face, and were generous with invitations to eat with their families. The men gave her the same respect they would give to an Englishwoman, treating her with great courtesy.

Having sworn to present a good image of Russia, and being a proud woman herself, Galina did not allow herself to give the slightest hint that she was hungry. She simply accepted the invitations with gratitude and with grace.

Her first months in Senenga were like a big jigsaw whose pattern she couldn't yet see. She tried to concentrate on the things that mattered: to give good maths lessons, to survive and not to appear ignorant.

Galina felt like a sponge, absorbing everything. Trying to cope with a new environment and a new language, it was some time before she could start to look at people as individuals. It was a very difficult time for her. And throughout this difficult time, this Englishman called Peter kept making remarks about her leaving 'propaganda' around the staffroom.

Try as she might, it was impossible not to notice him. He was big, he was loud, and he was always the centre of attention in the staffroom and in the bar. He lived in a very open way, and there always seemed to be crowds of people going in and out of his house. He laughed a lot, and when he had stayed too long down at the bar you could hear his lion-roar all over the compound as he thundered his way back to his house.

She didn't think he meant to be unkind, but he seemed to enjoy teasing her. Sometimes his remarks were mild and general, maybe a smiling reminder to 'pick up her bits and pieces'. Sometimes, though, she felt they were much more pointed.

One evening, when she was sitting with Myra Harrison at a table in the bar, he brought his beer over and sat down beside her.

'I've just remembered something that might interest you,' he said. 'Did you know there's a legend that Moscow was founded by the grandson of an English king?' He laughed. 'Maybe you and I are distant cousins, who knows? Everybody keeps saying what a small world it is.' He threw his head back and laughed even louder.

Galina wasn't sure if she understood what he was saying. She found his accent very difficult. To her ears, he sounded as if he was speaking with a potato in his mouth.

'What is this – cousins? I do not understand. Please, speak more slowly.'

He went on as if she hadn't said a word, 'Yes, it's true. Prince ... I think it was "Monomake", but I'm not sure ... anyway, he was a prince of Kiev and he married Gytha, the daughter of our Harold the Second – the one that got the arrow in the eye at Hastings, you might remember. They had a son called Longarm, and he was the one who founded Moscow ... d'you follow?'

Galina was completely lost by this time. Was Peter drunk? Or was he teasing her again? She was relieved when he gave up and went back to his friends.

'Don't let Peter worry you,' Myra said. 'He's all right. He's like a big friendly bear, really. He just likes talking to people.'

Maybe, Galina thought, but I wish he wouldn't pick on me.

Another evening, they were playing cards at Myra Harrison's house and he looked across the table and asked her casually, 'Did you know that your hero Karl Marx is buried in London?'

She didn't know that, but she said nothing.

Myra said, 'Come on, Peter, stop teasing Galina. You know she's shy.'

She wasn't shy, she just didn't want to talk about Russia. But the Englishman wouldn't leave her alone.

'It's absolutely true. He's pushing up the daisies in Highgate Cemetery. And he never did go to Russia. I never could figure out why Russia's so keen on his ideas.'

How she wished Alex was still here. He would know how to handle this. Clearly this man was trying to provoke her into an argument. For a moment, she was tempted to take up the challenge. But she bit her lip. She couldn't answer him back. Her orders were to keep a low profile and do what she had been sent to do.

*

40

The table in the staffroom was often littered with tracts bearing messages from 'The Respected and Beloved leader Kim Il Sung'. Kim Il Sung, someone explained, was some kind of Korean guru. Galina had no idea who was leaving this material.

The brochures she had orders to distribute were not overtly propagandist. They were designed to promote goodwill towards Russia. Glossy and attractive, they were mostly about the University of Patrice Lumumba and were full of pictures of black and white students walking, talking and playing sport together in a very friendly manner.

There was a strong emphasis on 'Friendship between peoples', and on encouraging students from Africa and Asia to come to Russia to study under 'very favourable conditions'. There were also articles about the Russian health service, the best in the world, Russian art, also the best in the world, about Moscow and Leningrad, where the buildings, too, were the best in the world. According to these brochures, everything in the USSR was far better than anything they would find anywhere in the West.

Galina left the Korean leaflets where they were and quietly placed some of her own brochures on top. The parcels of brochures kept arriving. They came by every post, from the Embassy and the trading posts and the mission.

Perhaps she was naïve in the extreme, but she didn't see her actions as particularly subversive. This was just something she had to do. At the briefing before the teachers left Moscow, they were instructed not to push anything into people's hands but simply to leave the material lying around.

If the African teachers were sitting in the staffroom with nothing much to do, they might pick up the brochures and ask questions. The Russian teachers were then to tell them how wonderful everything in Russia was, and what good friends of the African people the Russians were.

Still Galina's belongings didn't come. Still her salary didn't come. But still the booklets continued to come.

Galina's colleagues in the maths department tried to look after her, and several other families treated her with great kindness.

41

One Sri Lankan family made sure she ate regularly. If she didn't come to their house for dinner, they sent over a houseboy with a meal for her.

Every morning, she found a Zambian sitting on her front step. The plea was always the same: 'Madam, take me as your houseboy.' If only they knew. She had less money in her pocket than most of the expats paid their houseboys every week.

No one on the teaching staff had the slightest idea of the predicament Galina was in. She never said a word to anyone about the way she was having to live. She was hungry all the time and beginning to lose weight, but she would have died rather than ask for help.

She had been sent to Zambia to show that she, a Russian, was a better teacher than any of the other nationals, and to help convince the Africans that Russia was more friendly to them than any other country, particularly any Western country.

If she failed to do this it could mean the end of her contract. The fact that there were no other Russians closer than Mongu made no difference. She had grown up believing that there were watchers everywhere, even where you could see none. If you gave the slightest sign of misbehaviour, the authorities would know somehow.

Galina admitted a long time later that, in fact, the Russians generally did not like Africans at all. Russia had a far higher proportion of racists than any other nationality. They despised black people. They considered them inferior and dirty, and openly called them 'black-arses'.

Individually, Russians only came to Africa for the money, for the currency roubles. The much-prized privilege of working in Zambia carried with it an obligation to spread, casually and unobtrusively, as much propaganda material as they could. This material mainly came in the form of glossy brochures full of beautiful pictures of Moscow, the kind of material Galina was receiving.

The USSR saw Zambia as a particularly plum prize, with its advantageous geo-political position and the valuable mineral resources of the Copper Belt. This was why only the best and most trusted teachers were sent there.

In Muscovite society, however, it was no secret that black Africans who took the propaganda at face value and came to the university had a very hard time. The Russian students routinely abused them, kicked them and beat them up. If a black student was foolish or daring enough to invite a white woman to dance, he would be thrashed, and a white Russian woman could do nothing more shameful than to marry a black man. They would be ostracized utterly.

There was absolutely no public tolerance of blacks. Galina knew of very few cases where any Russian married a black African. The apartheid regime in South Africa was relaxed in comparison.

But here she was, behaving with typical Russian double standards, distributing literature she did not believe in because her contract – and her currency roubles – depended on following the instructions she had been given. She had sworn to obey orders, and she knew that failure to do so would result in a very fast trip home.

I neither knew nor suspected any of this at the time. I hadn't the slightest inkling, either, of the difficult living conditions Galina was having to cope with. But this quiet, attractive woman intrigued me. She never responded to my jokes, and I could never work out why. Even while I was teasing her I realized it was a ham-fisted kind of approach, but I couldn't think of any other way to break through the barriers she seemed determined to set up.

Maybe she didn't understand, but then again maybe she did. Or maybe she just didn't like me. I had no way of telling. She would simply look at me with those dark eyes that saw everything and showed nothing.

By the end of that term I knew very little more about her than when she first arrived in Senanga. To get to know her better I would have had to spend a lot more time with her, and time was always scarce in my busy life.

I went home on leave for Christmas 1975, home to family and friends and the customary celebrations, without the slightest notion that when I returned to Zambia a few weeks later my life would change for ever.

7

Senanga, Zambia: January 1976

I was busy unpacking my bags when Myra came over to my house to tell me that Galina had been involved in a very serious road accident just before Christmas, and had spent the weeks since then in the district hospital at Mongu.

She was out of danger now, but had suffered severe concussion, several broken ribs, and injuries to her back. Myra thought it unlikely that Galina would be up to teaching for some time to come.

'Dr Dashko was driving,' Myra said. 'You know Viktor Dashko, don't you? He wasn't hurt himself, but his wife and Galina were both badly injured. I understand they're out of hospital now, and he's looking after Galina in his own house.'

'I'll drive over tomorrow,' I said. 'I'll try to find out when she'll be well enough to come back here. Then we'll need to arrange for someone to ferry her over. I suppose it'll all be down to us.'

Damned Russians. They still hadn't sent a teacher to replace Alex, and now this! We were going to be even more short-staffed. I still blush with shame to remember the thoughts that raced through my mind that day. How on earth was I going to re-jig the timetable to cover Galina's absence? It would be a last resort, but I might even have to take her classes in with mine.

Last term, I'd had to readjust everything to accommodate her presence. Now I was going to have to compensate for her absence. This woman was upsetting the comfortable routine of my life.

Before I had time to make the trip to Mongu, two of the nuns from our school arrived in the compound with Galina stretched out prone in the back of their van. Sister Carmel and Sister Bernadette had been on one of their regular visits to the hospital at Mongu, and when they learned that Galina was fit enough to travel back to Senanga they offered to bring her.

The road from Mongu had not been improved. It was still the rutted and pot-holed dirt track I knew so well. The journey must have been a nightmare for Galina, a long painful rattle and roll through choking dust and sweltering heat.

By the time the Sisters and I had helped her get down to stand in her dusty sandals on the even dustier ground outside her house she was biting back tears. She tried to convince us she could manage on her own, but we took no notice of her. She looked pathetically weak and ill, and the slightest movement made her wince.

It also registered at some more personal level of my mind that Galina had lost a great deal of weight. In our fairly casual acquaintance, I had not consciously assessed her physical attributes. You could say I hadn't noticed her much at all, except as a competent teacher who didn't speak very good English and who kept cluttering the staffroom with travel brochures.

But unless my memory was playing me tricks, she was far thinner now than she had been before I'd gone away for the Christmas holidays. Her cotton dress hung in loose folds around her body. The dress had once been blue, but was now so faded its colour was only a vague memory. There was a waif-like aura about her, and it was compassion more than anything that moved me to lift her in my arms and carry her into the house.

This was the first time I'd been in this house since Galina moved in the previous September. She never invited anyone to visit her, and I didn't need more than a glance around to realize why. Apart from bits of basic furniture and a few shabby rugs I recognized as relics of the previous tenant, the house was bare.

Lowering Galina as gently as possible on to one of the two chairs in the room, I saw she was weeping silent tears. Something told me her distress was caused as much by embarrassment as by physical pain. I pretended not to notice, and walked into the kitchen, intending to make her a cool drink. She certainly needed some kind of refreshment after that hellish journey.

I could hardly believe what I saw in that kitchen. An ancient wood-burning stove blackened from years of use, a bare wooden table, a couple of kitchen chairs, empty shelves ... on the cooker, a battered saucepan and a rusty-rimmed tin mug ... in one corner, a paraffin stove even more decrepit than the wood-burner.

It was a very small kitchen, and its walls were streaked black with soot that clung like mucky cobwebs. A box of matches lay on the floor. I picked it up, thinking I might try to boil up some water. Every match in the box had been split down the middle to make two ...

Dear God ... how could anyone live like this? Particularly, how could a woman live like this? For three months, and in a climate like this ... No fridge, no stores, the only food in the cupboard a single shrivelled pineapple ...

It was difficult enough to keep a place clean here, even with the help of a houseboy. Dust, smoke and creepy-crawlies got everywhere. Galina must have been struggling all these months without any help, without even the most basic equipment.

None of the other teachers in Senanga lived in such awful conditions. Africans, Indians, Europeans ... while the pay didn't run to luxurious living, the expats here lived in reasonable comfort. Our 'cuisine' might not be cordon bleu, or even remotely interesting, but there was plenty of food around. It had never crossed my mind that anyone might be living in our school compound in such truly terrible circumstances.

I wanted to remove Galina bodily across the compound to my own house, but quickly thought better of that idea. She was upset enough. To attract the attention of the entire compound by doing anything so dramatic would be more cruel than kind.

'Stay there!' I saw her flinch, but it was too late to lighten the gruff tone with which the order came out of my constricted throat. It was probably an unnecessary growl anyway. I don't think she could have moved, she was so exhausted after that awful bone-jarring ride from Mongu.

I headed for Myra's house. Halfway there, it struck me that asking Myra for help might distress Galina even more. Clearly, she hadn't wanted anyone to know what she had been enduring since her arrival in Senanga. She wouldn't have kept quiet otherwise. I would be doing her no favours by broadcasting her problems. There had to be a better way. Something had to be done quickly, though, and as Galina was under me on the school staff, in my book that something was down to me.

I went to my house and collected a bottle of lemonade from my fridge. Then I packed a holdall with goodies I'd brought back from my leave, tinned red salmon, crispbreads, a tin of butter and some shortbread biscuits, plus a couple of cups, plates, spoons and knives.

At that time, I was sharing the house with a Zambian teacher called Blyson Kahela, but luckily he was out. I didn't call for my houseboy to help carry the stuff – it would be better not to give the locals any cause for speculation or, even worse, gossip.

That was the first meal I shared with Galina. She ate little, and very slowly. She apologized for her lack of appetite. 'I have eaten hardly any food since the accident. This is very good, very nice, the lemonade.' She managed a smile with the words.

She had made polite noises about refusing to accept the things I'd brought, but she was too weak to protest with any conviction. She drank the lemonade as if she'd never tasted anything so good. I was pleased about that, as I'd made it myself from fresh lemons.

I promised to bring another bottle later, and left her to rest.

There were a thousand and one things to do at the school, getting organized for the new term, which was due to start in a couple of days. I didn't find time to go to Galina's house again till the evening. She had managed to sleep for a couple of hours, she told me. She certainly looked a little better than she had when I left her.

As well as the promised lemonade, I had brought a flask of boiled water and a jar of the instant coffee I kept for those occasions when it was too much bother to make 'proper coffee'. We drank coffee and ate biscuits, and Galina tried to explain what had happened to her and why she was in so much trouble.

'I had to get to Lusaka,' she said. 'I had to get to our Embassy. You remember Alex had to go home, his feet were so bad. Now I am alone. I know everyone tries to be kind but, you see, we are not supposed to talk to foreigners except in working, in teaching. It is not allowed.'

Her eyes were dark and serious. They watched me intently as she went on, 'I am breaking my promise to the State by talking to you about these things. But now, like this – ' she indicated her injured body ' – I do not think I can live without help.'

'Of course I'll help. I'll do anything I can. Just tell me what I can do?'

'Thank you, Peter. But please – promise me you won't tell anyone else what it is like here in this house.' She made a helpless little gesture at the primitive conditions around us. 'I do not want charity. Soon everything will get better. Soon my money will come. It has all been a terrible mistake, but soon everything will be sorted out.'

Galina's hands were clenched tight. I was beginning to realize what it was costing this proud woman to ask for my help – for anyone's help. She had been living in squalor since the day she arrived in Senanga, and had confided in no one. Now she had no choice.

So I gave my word, and listened in silence as she spoke in her soft heavily accented voice. 'I had to get to Lusaka to find out what had happened to my luggage. I have no belongings – you can see.' She looked around the comfortless room.

'I came with nothing. Everything was left at the airport in Moscow. Our Embassy promised to find it, but nothing has happened. I need also to find out where my money is. Since I came here nobody has sent my salary. I have no money to buy food or anything else, only forty kwachas I was given in Lusaka when I came. Since that, nothing. There has been some administrative mistake, of course, some error of communication. Our people always look after us.'

I was beginning to wonder about that, but it was none of my business to say so.

'So I am waiting for my situation to be sorted out. Then Doctor Dashko, he comes from Lusaka to see the nuns, so I ask please will he take me to the Embassy. I go to find my luggage and my salary, and I will spend the holidays with friends from Russia who are living in Lusaka, my friend L and his wife.

'We would not celebrate Christmas, that means nothing to us, but we would celebrate the Russian New Year on the seventh day of January. If I can get to Lusaka, my life in Africa will be much better, and I will be having a happy time with my friends.

'But I have no vehicle, no money for the bus, no way to get there. So Doctor Dashko takes me in his car, but he must go first to the hospital in Kaoma to pick up his wife.

'When the wife is in the car we leave. We are only a short time out of Kaoma on the road to Lusaka when something happens. I am not sure what it was, but I think we have to avoid some very old man on a bike who comes suddenly out of the dust. Then our vehicle is off the road and turning over three or four times. After that I don't remember much, only darkness and pain.

'Doctor Dashko is shocked and bruised, but he's okay. We were not going fast, it was such a bad road, so that saved us. His wife was hurt as well as me. He tells me a lorry-driver passing saw the accident and stopped and brought us all on the back of his lorry to the hospital in Kaoma.

'In Kaoma hospital we have emergency jabs – you know, tetanus and antibiotic and pain-killers, all those things. I am unconscious and they can't take my dress off, they have to cut it off. But the hospital at Kaoma is not a real hospital, it's only a clinic really, so we have to be moved to the hospital in Mongu to have proper treatment.'

'You mean they moved you 110 miles? In such a terrible state?' I had worked in Kaoma, and I knew the road they must have travelled. It was every bit as primitive as the road from Mongu to Senanga, unmade, rough, rutted and full of potholes. The journey must have been agony.

'There was nothing else to do. They lifted us on to the back of the lorry, and the driver took us to the hospital in Mongu.'

I could hardly take in what she was telling me. The pictures her words painted were all too stark in my mind. 110 miles over that terrible road, injured, and bumped about in the back of a lorry. 'You must have gone through hell!'

'There was nothing else to do,' she shrugged, and winced with the movement. 'Anyway, I was not conscious most of the time. Once or twice I came round, but there was such pain I passed out again. I didn't care what happened then, only that I wouldn't feel the pain . . .'

Her voice was dropping, although I could see she wanted to go on. This was probably the first time she had talked with any degree of openness for months. But exhaustion was dulling her eyes and, much as I wanted to hear the whole story, I knew she had had enough. She'd had a long exhausting day, and she needed rest more than she needed to talk.

I promised to come back the next evening.

I kept my promise, and as soon as Galina opened the door to let me in, it was obvious she was in just as much discomfort as yesterday, perhaps even more, for she held herself as if her muscles had stiffened up. Every move she made looked agonizing, and it took her several minutes just to lower herself inch by inch on to a chair. She waved me away when I tried to help.

Her voice was stronger, though, and it didn't take me long to realize she had dropped some kind of curtain between us. Discipline and training had taken over. Pride ruled again. She wanted only the barest essentials of help from me, and, she insisted, from no one else.

I made a simple meal which we shared, but the easy intimacy of yesterday evening had gone. After half an hour I left, baffled and, yes, even a little hurt.

Something was going on here, something I didn't understand. Our conversation tonight had been formal, with none of the companionship we had shared yesterday, not as friends exactly, but as colleagues. My tentative attempt to get Galina to continue where she left off had been met with a shrug and a dismissive 'Don't worry, I'll be okay.'

I felt shut out, and I didn't like it.

Before heading for home, I went to look for the nuns who had brought Galina from Mongu. The Sisters taught Religious Instruction and Domestic Science at the school, and we always had a nun as housemistress to look after our girl pupils.

I wasn't sure why I wanted to do this, but I needed to talk to someone. I needed to know what had really happened to Galina. Part of it, perhaps subconscious at this time, was also a need to understand what made this enigmatic woman tick. She was altogether too proud for her own good.

I found Sister Bernadette coming out of one of the classrooms. Good. This most serene of women would surely know something about what had gone on in the hospital in Mongu. Before she went silent on me, Galina had told me the quiet Sister had spent a lot of time with her while she was confined to bed. The nun would never betray confidences, I knew, but if I could get her to talk to me even a little, it might help.

'May I talk to you, please, Sister? In private, just for a few minutes? It's about Galina Vasilyeva.'

Sister Bernadette led me back into the empty classroom. It wasn't the most comfortable of places, but at least no one could overhear. The Sister listened to my questions, looking straight into my eyes as I spoke. She seemed to be assessing me, weighing up my motives, perhaps.

'You're right, of course,' she said. 'Galina Vasilyeva is a touch too proud for her own good, as you say. She told me very little, as a matter of fact, but I saw a lot. Believe me, if it wasn't for her pride and a great deal of determination, she wouldn't be alive today. That was a terrible accident she had, truly terrible. She was lucky to survive.

'They hit something on the road. Nobody is sure what it was, but Doctor Dashko lost control of the car. They went off the road and rolled over three or four times. That's all Galina can remember.'

I said, 'Yes, she told me about the accident. She talked to me last night. She was very tired, very weak, and she was obviously in a great deal of pain. She's lost a terrific amount of weight, too, anyone can see that. But today . . . she seems stronger and she's trying to be cheerful, but she doesn't want to talk about her problems – and goodness knows she's got plenty of those.'

'I can only tell you what I know. You must take what you can from it. And I'm not breaking any confidences – everybody at the hospital knew what was going on. I can see you're anxious about her. So are we all, but she keeps us at arm's length.'

So Sister Bernadette told me what she could.

Galina lay in the hospital all through Christmas, helpless and in almost constant pain from her injuries in spite of heavy medication. Anyone who has suffered broken ribs will know it's no picnic.

She also had cystitis from an inadequately sterilized catheter. This painful infection made her want to pass urine frequently, and each time she did so she suffered half an hour of screaming agony, worse even than the pain from her broken ribs.

Dr Dashko worked in this hospital, and managed to arrange a special ward for his wife and Galina. At least they had a little more peace and quiet there than in a general ward.

The nuns did their best to make the festival a happy time. Someone found a small artificial Christmas tree from goodness knows where, and the nuns made improvized decorations from different coloured pills. Sister Bernadette laughed as she remembered how they put a suppository at the top of the tree as a stand-in for the star they didn't have. She made the whole thing sound like fun, describing how the nuns coped with such limited resources.

Then one day in January, two officials from the Russian

Embassy in Lusaka arrived at the hospital. Dr Dashko told Galina the Embassy was sending someone to make enquiries about the accident, and Galina told the nuns these officials would be bringing her salary and her belongings, everything that had been missing since she left Moscow. So she waited for the visit. And waited ... and waited ...

Oh yes, the officials from the Embassy did come, Sister Bernadette said. The nuns heard from Viktor Dashko exactly what happened then.

The Russians arrived in the middle of the afternoon. They brought bottles of vodka and packs of cigarettes, and they headed first for the police station, then for the hospital office. They made extensive enquiries at both places, and were obviously very keen to establish where the responsibility lay for what had happened.

They learned that the accident had been just that, an unfortunate accident, and that the person driving the car was a Russian. They satisfied themselves that no prosecution or any other action would be brought against the embassy.

Most important of all, they checked thoroughly to make sure no one was involved who might try to make a claim for damages, a claim that might deplete Russian currency reserves. Then they left.

The officials did not visit Galina. They did not bring her belongings, or her salary. They did not enquire about her health, her well-being or her ability to resume her work. They simply drove away.

Sister Bernadette said, 'So now you see why she doesn't want to ask for help. She simply can't understand why her own people have done this to her, why they don't seem the slightest bit interested in her.'

I tried to imagine how Galina must be feeling. She was a good Russian. She was a good teacher. She was a woman alone in a foreign country, and she had been so sure the people at her Embassy would look after her. No wonder she was putting up barriers. She must feel utterly bewildered and humiliated. And utterly alone.

*

The first day of the new term arrived. I got over to the school early and found Galina there before me, ready to take her class as usual.

The staff were delighted to see her, of course. Everyone knew she had been in an accident. But I was certain no one but me knew what it had cost her to get here. No one else had seen her take a full five minutes to raise herself from lying flat to a sitting position, then another ten to stand upright.

How she dragged herself from her house to the school through that clogging carpet of dust I'll never know. But here she was, on her feet, on time, and determined to carry on as usual. From that moment, I had the greatest respect for Galina Vasilyeva.

It took a while, and I didn't push, but eventually Galina agreed to come with me down to the bar on the riverbank. She was still wary about socializing, and I thought maybe she felt self-conscious about her clothes, which she must know were looking pretty shabby by now. But everybody went out of their way to make her welcome, and over the next few weeks she gradually relaxed a little.

She began to join in some of the card games that were a regular part of the evening's entertainment. We played a lot of tarot, which she seemed to enjoy, and I discovered she was an excellent chess player. We had some pretty fierce battles over the chess board.

She even found enough confidence to speak up in defence of her country on one or two occasions, when she caught unflattering remarks about the Soviets and their activities in the Cold War. There was no doubt Galina loved her country, however shabbily they might be treating her right now.

8

Senanga, Zambia: March 1976

There was a constant stream of visitors at my house. In my seven years in Africa I had met hundreds of people in all kinds of work and always honoured the hospitable tradition among expats. Every passing traveller knew he'd be welcome to stop over at my place.

More often than not my house, especially my kitchen, was full of people tucking into whatever culinary delicacy happened to be on the menu. I'm an enthusiastic cook, but my repertoire was far from extensive, and the range of ingredients available locally was pretty limited. Curry, curry, or curry was the usual choice. And always with rice.

As Galina slowly recovered, I began to invite her more and more often to come and share meals at my house. Sometimes we were on our own, sometimes there was a crowd. As the weeks went by, she began to spend more time in my house than in her own. I was getting used to having her around, and as her English improved I began to appreciate her quiet sense of humour.

Although Blyson Kahela and I jogged along reasonably well, we led completely different lives and sometimes we got on each other's nerves. We more or less kept out of each other's way, and he always made himself scarce when Galina was visiting.

Galina began to make jokes about my rice and the curry stew I made from the local Barotse beef. Dessert was nearly always pawpaw in some form or other, which she hinted was just a shade boring. Maybe Galina had a point, but my life was too

56

busy for elaborate cooking. Anyway, in my view, there are few foods more delicious than pawpaw. It's soft and sweet and smooth as a peach, with a taste I can only describe as a cross between a peach and a melon.

I was very proud of my method of tenderizing the beef. I wrapped it in the leaves of the papaya tree or in the skin of the papaya fruit. The locals told me this tree contains a protein-digesting enzyme which is very effective in rendering even Barotse beef palatable. Without the papaya treatment, this beef retains the famous texture of old shoe-leather, however long you cook it.

I'd read somewhere that a migrating Bantu people from the north first brought cattle into the area around the Sixth century AD. There were times when the local beef was so tough you could be forgiven for suspecting it might have come from the original herd.

I had all sorts of ways of serving mango, too. If you cut it up and bake it in pastry, mango makes quite an acceptable 'apple' pie. Unripe mango tastes a bit like raw apple, and you can cut it like chips and eat it fresh. My cuisine might not have thrilled Fanny Craddock, but given the circumstances I didn't think it was too bad.

Galina was getting stronger by the day, and we were gradually getting to know each other better, both of us letting the barriers drop a little, I suppose. She was feeling a lot happier now, because at long last her belongings had arrived and her salary was coming through.

One day, she invited me to come to her house for a meal. She was obviously pleased to be able to do this, to return, as she put it, 'a tiny bit of the generous hospitality' I'd given her since her accident. She said she felt too shy to ask any of the other teachers yet, but maybe sometime soon . . .

Galina had never boasted about her cooking, but the wonderful meal she served me that evening made me wonder how she had put up with my own efforts for so long. She gave me a kind of burger made from ground beef, which I could hardly believe came from the same source as the 'prime cuts' we were used to risking our teeth on. She had filled a soft baked bun with the meat and, whatever kind of magic she had worked on it, the whole thing just melted in my mouth. It was absolutely wonderful.

Galina watched me eat. When she saw what pleasure her food was giving me she positively beamed with satisfaction. It wasn't only the food I was enjoying, of course, it was the whole experience, the elegant way Galina served the meal, the little feminine touches like the linen napkins and tablecloth, her conversation, her company. This was all so different from the haphazard bachelor meals I was used to. Maybe I had been missing something all these years.

When we'd eaten every crumb, I persuaded Galina to walk down to the bar with me. For some reason, it suddenly seemed very important to show her the sunset over the river. In all the months she had been in Senanga, keeping herself to herself and hardly ever leaving the school compound, she could never have had the thrill of seeing the sun set on the Zambezi.

We walked at a gentle pace on the dirt path, taking care not to overtax Galina's strength. As we strolled towards the river the sun was just touching the horizon. Our long thin black shadows followed us along the path, and we laughed together at the way my pointed head stretched for yards behind Galina's.

Every few steps, we stopped to gaze entranced at the great red-gold ball that hung in the evening sky. All the glorious colours of the sunset rippled in the water, turning it to liquid gold dappled with the black silhouettes of drifting boats. We tried to put names to the colours we were looking at, and Galina struggled with her English to find the words she wanted.

'Golden fire,' she offered.

'Beaten purple bronze,' I countered.

'Melted lava.'

'Liquid copper . . .'

But this breathtaking African sunset was far too beautiful to describe in words, and we both fell silent.

Galina slipped her hand into mine as we walked, almost as if she needed to be reassured she wasn't dreaming. When we reached the riverbank we stood together at the edge of the water, marvelling at the changing reflections as the great crimson globe began to slide into the skyline.

We watched as the sun slowly changed shape to a glowing half-moon, a fat crescent, an eyebrow. Then there was darkness, as black and sudden as if someone had switched off a light. We could see nothing, not even each other.

Without a word and still hand-in-hand, we made our way through the night towards the lights and noise of the riverside bar. The usual crowd crammed the place, and all our fellow expat teachers were there. Nobody showed the slightest surprise when Galina and I walked in together.

They all knew we visited each other, of course. We had never tried to hide this. They knew I was looking after her, and it was to me they addressed their enquiries about her welfare. Rather to my surprise, I found myself accepting the role of protector quite comfortably.

We had a few drinks, and moved around chatting with various friends, straining to hear ourselves speak above the hubbub of voices and the drumming throb of the music, but we didn't stay long. It was as though we both wanted to hold on to the closeness we had found walking together in that glorious sunset.

The night seemed intensely dark and hushed after the bright hard lights and the racket inside the bar. A memory from my schooldays surfaced in my mind. It was Dylan Thomas, wasn't it, who described a night in a Welsh valley as 'Bible-black'. That was it exactly, 'Bible-black' fitted this night perfectly. It felt so quiet, so peaceful, so right, being here with Galina.

I put my arm around her shoulders, and as we walked together she relaxed against me and let me draw her closer. Our steps became slower and slower, till we stopped walking and I put my arms around her. There in the quiet warmth of the African night, filled with magical memories of the sunset we had shared, we kissed for the first time.

Galina and I were growing closer, but in my mind at least our relationship was still quite casual. Perhaps neither of us was ready to make any kind of firm commitment, and we were

59

happy to let things drift along. We enjoyed spending time together and generally getting to know each other. Perhaps, too, there were thoughts at the back of our minds which we didn't want to acknowledge, thoughts about the problems a closer involvement might bring.

It made a tremendous difference to my life, knowing Galina. Most of my colleagues were married, and at the end of a sociable evening at the bar or someone's house, off they'd go back to their own quarters. For me, it was usually a lonely bunk-down at ten o'clock when the lights went out. This was in no sense a curfew, simply a practical measure to conserve our erratic energy supply, but if you wanted to stay up after 'Lights-out' you had to have the Tilley lamp ready or resort to candles.

I spent many long happy evenings with Galina, playing chess or tarot by candle-light. We talked non-stop, about life in general and our own lives in particular.

Galina's tastes were firmly on the classical side, which didn't surprise me when she described her education. She read Tolstoy, Dostoevsky and Turgenev, while my reading leaned towards Wilbur Smith or Alistair Maclean, with a dash of Louis L'Amour or Zane Grey. She loved Tchaikovsky, Rachmaninov, Paganini, and she adored Bizet's *Carmen*. I tapped my feet to the Rolling Stones, Herman's Hermits and the Beatles. Galina had never heard of the Beatles.

Other than our profession we had nothing in common, yet I enjoyed her company enormously. She had an inner happiness that coloured everything she said and did, a joyous spirit and a love of life I found very attractive. She took enormous pleasure in the simplest things, like cooking a meal together. It was a joy to be with her. My life was a lot more interesting, and a lot more fun.

At the same time, Galina was beginning to mix more freely with the other members of staff. She was on particularly friendly terms with one of the Pakistani families who had helped her survive after Alex went home, while completely unaware of how vital their friendship was.

Some of the men who were living in the school compound found Galina very attractive, and made no pretence about it. They paid her lavish compliments, and I couldn't blame them for that. One day, however, one man overstepped the mark. This man was an Indian who had come to Senanga without his wife. Perhaps he was lonely, but that was no excuse for his behaviour, not in my book anyway.

Galina's Pakistani friends were going to dinner at the local hospital, and invited her to go with them. The Indian teacher was also a guest, and he drove them all in his car.

Over dinner, when he was in no danger of being overheard in the din of conversation and laughter, this man began to make highly suggestive remarks to Galina. He was very direct, and offered to introduce her to the wonders of the *Kama Sutra*. He was very experienced, he promised her, in the finer aspects of its text. The Indian was a very smooth talker, and did his honey-tongued best to convince Galina he was the man who could show her the best sex in the world.

Galina parried his advances as best she could. The last thing she wanted was to make a scene and embarrass the couple whose guest she was. As the plates were changed and the glasses refilled, the Indian became bolder and bolder, and so did his language.

Eventually Galina told him quietly, 'But I don't want just sex. I want love. And you can't give me that, even if you wanted to. You have a wife already.'

Any hope that a mention of the man's wife would shut him up vanished as soon as he opened his mouth again. Resistance was only adding spice to the chase.

Galina was becoming more and more embarrassed. She was not an innocent young girl, but this man was going far beyond the pale, and she knew her English was not up to an effective put-down. She could have squashed him dead in Russian.

Fortunately, the Pakistani wife had noticed her discomfort. This Indian had acquired a less than savoury reputation where women were concerned, and Galina's friend quickly realized what was happening. She whispered something to her husband, who glanced briefly across the table then quietly excused himself. He slipped out of the building, found a boy and sent him running back to the township to look for me.

The boy found me in my house, working on papers for the next day's classes. The poor fellow had run so fast he was gasping for breath, and he didn't make a lot of sense at first, but I soon picked up the gist of what he was saying. Miss Vasilyeva had trouble at the hospital – that was enough for me. I dropped my papers on the table and ran the two miles up the dirt road to the hospital, leaving the winded boy far behind.

When I got to the hospital, the meal was just finishing. I stood in the doorway and looked round the tables till I spotted Galina. I had no problem locating her. There are times when it's a great advantage to be taller than average.

Her Pakistani friends must have been watching for me. They saw me at once and signalled my presence to Galina. In the general noise of conversation and clattering of dishes, nobody else noticed Galina leave the table. Taking her move as an invitation, her Indian beau followed her, flashing his teeth in a delighted smile.

The sight of me waiting in the foyer wiped the smile right off his face. He knew very well who I was, and as he was half my size he decided the wisest course was to act the innocent.

'I think perhaps Miss Vasilyeva is not feeling very well. She needs some air . . .' It would be unkind to say he grovelled, but he came close to it.

I looked at Galina, but she indicated there was nothing wrong with her and made a gesture of disgust towards the Indian.

'Where's your car?' I growled at the man.

'Over there.' He waved a hand at the courtyard.

'Okay,' I said, and moved in that direction. 'Come on, then. You're driving!'

Gathering his dignity around him, but plainly highly offended, the man got into his car and drove us back to Galina's house. The journey didn't take very long, but it was long enough for me to realise that the outrage I was feeling was a lot worse than anger. It was jealousy. It had hit me like a punch in the gut when I saw this fellow get up grinning and follow

Galina. For a few terrible seconds I thought she had actually come to the dinner with this man as her partner. And I suddenly knew I couldn't cope with that.

When we got to her house Galina and I got out, and I ordered the fellow straight back to the dinner, otherwise the Pakistani couple would have to find another lift home.

'You're talking to me as if I'm a driver, not a teacher,' he grumbled. But he had calmed down a bit by now and the anger had gone from his voice. He looked out of the car, first at me then at Galina.

'I can see he really loves you,' he said and drove away.

I made sure Galina was safely inside her house, then walked to my own place. It was a long time before sleep came. There was an awful lot to think about.

How could this have happened to me, the footloose, fancy-free gung-ho bachelor? Oh sure, I'd had a few girlfriends over the years, but nothing you could really call a close relationship. There always seemed to be more interesting things to do.

But this woman had somehow got under my skin. Something had been happening to me over these past weeks, something I'd been too busy to notice. It had crept up on me while I wasn't looking. And if the jealous rage that had nearly burned me up this evening was anything to go by, that something must surely be love.

My last thought before sleep came was that maybe, just maybe, my bachelor days might be coming to an end.

9

Senanga, Zambia: April 1976

My houseboy arrived unannounced on Galina's doorstep.
'*Bwana* ask I bring this to you.' 'This' was my refrigerator.
'But what is happening? What does it mean?'
'*Bwana* says he will live here.'
I had decided to move into Galina's house. This probably looks like colossal presumption, and maybe it was, but I had absolutely no doubt it was the right thing for both of us. I also decided on surprise tactics as the best way to save hours, maybe days or even weeks, convincing Galina. We were good for each other, and she needed someone around. And I never wanted to feel that jealous agony again.
My cooker came next, then my deep freeze. All day my servant was in and out, carrying my cooking gear, my dinner service, my stocks of food . . .
So Galina and I began to live together openly in her house.

I promised to teach Galina the British way of life. She must have thought it very odd when the first thing I taught her was how to make curry. This was because friends were constantly coming and going, and they always needed feeding.
Our visitors were mostly engineers from the Livingstone Public Works Department, whose job it was to maintain machinery, water pumps and the like throughout the territory. We also had teachers passing through from other townships, and sometimes there would be Yugoslavs doing maintenance and building work nearby. On one famous occasion a whole

football team arrived without warning, staff from another school.

It might be hundreds of miles to the next stop, so anyone passing through always had a bed for the night. I had to feed them, so I fed them curry. What else could be cooked up fast and in such quantity?

One day we had a party of friends stopping for lunch as they were passing through Senanga. We knew about this visit in advance, and Galina suggested we cook something different. We consulted my small collection of cookery books. I had brought some of these from England, others had been left behind by staff long since gone home. In a book called *Round the World Cookery* we found a recipe for beef stew in ale with prunes. We had enough ingredients in hand to increase the quantities six times so there would be plenty for everyone.

I went to meet our guests at the usual watering hole, leaving Galina to put the finishing touches to the meal. She read the instruction 'Squeeze a lemon', multiplied by six and squeezed six lemons into the stew. Nobody noticed anything. For weeks afterwards, whenever anybody mentioned lemons we'd both get the giggles.

We had been together for only a week when a new Russian teacher arrived, the long-awaited replacement for the unfortunate Alex. It was almost as if we had thrown the dice and been rewarded with the Goushchins.

Vladimir Goushchin taught science, mainly physics. It was clear from the beginning that he thought he knew everything there was to know about the subject. In fact, this was far from the case. However, he did know a bit about chess, and this was useful to me, because I was trying to build up the school chess club.

Vladimir's wife, Svetlana, didn't teach at all. In fact, it soon became clear she was something of a recluse who seldom ventured out of their house at all. The new Russian couple settled in, and kept themselves to themselves, as all good Russians ought to do.

The trouble was that Galina no longer conformed. The

Goushchins must have been kept very busy, trying to keep up with all that was going on. It must have been plain to see that we, the expats, now included Galina as one of us. The Goushchins made no comment to anyone.

When I remarked on this, Galina said, 'That makes no difference. Just because they don't talk to anybody here, it doesn't mean they don't see what is happening. Can't you tell from their faces when they see us together? They don't approve of us. They will have instructions to report back to the Embassy in Lusaka.'

'Maybe they won't bother.'

Galina shook her head. 'You don't understand. They have their orders. If someone else reports about us and the Goushchins have failed to do it, they'll be in very deep trouble.'

'What kind of trouble? Would they be sent home? Wouldn't that be good riddance?'

'It's not so simple. They will have family back home, maybe children. Someone is sure to still be in the USSR who is important for them. Russian families abroad are never complete. Always one person at least stays at home. That way, they know what might happen if they don't obey orders.'

Galina's words were like a cold hand on the back of my neck.

'So there's nothing we can do?'

'Nothing. It won't be very long before the Embassy knows all about us. And they are not going to like it.'

'Then they'll have to lump it. I'm not moving out again. What can they do about it anyway?'

Galina was silent for a long moment before she answered.

'It is easy for you to say this. You are English. You can go where you want, do what you want. It is not like that for me. I am not like you. I am not English. I am not free to do as I wish. They can do anything they like. I have to do what they tell me.'

I tried to reassure her, but of course she was right. By bringing our relationship into the open we had put ourselves at the mercy of the Russians. We could only wait and see.

In an effort to get our life on to some kind of normal footing, despite the shadow of the Goushchins, I set about putting the garden in order. Galina hadn't been able to do anything about the garden herself and she couldn't afford to pay for help. We hired a garden boy, mainly because everything you try to grow in Africa needs to be constantly watered, and this takes up a lot of gardening time.

Throughout my time in Senanga I grew everything I could. It gave me a great sense of achievement to go into my garden and pick my own fruit and vegetables. Somehow they always tasted better than anything I could buy. I'd have a go at anything that might have a chance of growing in this hot and mostly dry climate.

I planted a fence round the house, intending to establish a mulberry hedge. You break branches off the mulberry trees and stick them in the ground, and with a bit of luck and a lot of water they'll root and grow and eventually come to fruit.

I grew pineapple – you chop off and plant the top, and after about three years you'll get a pineapple. I never stayed in one place long enough to see more than one pineapple in any one house.

You can grow bananas from shoots in about 18 months, and once the plants start to flower and fruit the shoots will be ready for the next generation and you won't have to wait so long for the next crop. These are not the same as the bananas you buy in the UK. We often picked our bananas green, chopped them into slices, and fried them in oil. They made a very acceptable substitute for potato crisps.

I tried strawberries, too. With plenty of watering they grew in great profusion, but you had to watch out for insects, which got at them very quickly. We were plagued, too, by enormous grasshoppers.

We produced avocado pear and guavas and lots of pawpaw, which were very easy to grow. I didn't bother with oranges or lemons, you could buy those in the market. We tried all sorts of vegetables, but these were never as successful as the fruit.

I set up a hydrophonic system, a bit like the ones they use in Egypt, and tried to grow plants in the house in water with added chemicals. The plants grew quite well, but the experiment failed because we couldn't get rid of the fruit fly, they just bred and bred. Tobacco was another of my failures, sadly. The plants grew profusely, but I never could find a way to cure them successfully.

One of my great pleasures at this time was to show Galina how fruits and vegetables grow. All through my boyhood I helped my grandfather in his garden, and it was second nature to me to plant and nurture things. Galina was a city girl, and she had never seen a vegetable or a fruit grown from cuttings or seed. To her, carrots and potatoes were things you bought from shops, supposing the shops had any to sell.

Here in Senanga, if you had any sense you learned to be as self-sufficient as you could.

Galina was intrigued by the way I saved absolutely everything that might possibly prove useful. Hammers, screws, fuses and fuse-wire, plugs, bits of wire, string ... everything was stored in tins and boxes, labelled and stacked on racks. Some people thought this eccentric, but if anything went wrong I could usually find the means to fix it.

One day, I remember, the deputy head came round to the house and saw this room full of stores.

'What's all this for?' he asked. He obviously thought it a huge joke, me keeping these supplies at all, let alone keeping them so methodically arranged.

Two weeks later he arrived at my door saying, 'I can't start my van. I don't know what's wrong with it.'

I went back to his house with him and had a look at the vehicle. One of his fuses wasn't working properly so I got one from my stores, replaced the dud one and started the engine up.

'That's why I keep a house full of knick-knacks,' I said.

At weekends we often took a boat and travelled a few miles upriver, sometimes just the two of us, sometimes with friends.

We usually found hippos. You had to be careful not to get too close to hippos, as they could turn a boat over just like that! They would suddenly appear quite close to the boat, open their mouths and give a great snort. They always made me very nervous.

From the river you could see weaver-bird nests hanging from the trees, remarkable structures, sometimes immense and housing a large colony. Weaver-birds are common throughout Africa. Their bodies are elongated, their beaks curved and slightly conical, and their plumage is brightly coloured, particularly at breeding time. There were web-footed divers, too, and plenty of wild geese.

The fishing around Senanga was always good, with shoals of bream and tiger-fish. You had to be very careful when you caught tiger-fish. If you brought them out alive, they'd chew your toes given half a chance.

Crocodiles rarely showed themselves, but there were always poisonous snakes around. They even got into the school sometimes. I never heard of a snake attacking anyone in the water but it was none too wise to swim around Senanga anyway. There was bilharzia in the stream as well as crocodiles.

Wherever we wandered on the river there were always children fishing from canoes on the banks. Here at Senanga, the famous 'mighty Zambezi' was our local village stream. It took me a long time to get used to that.

So the weeks passed in a haze of happiness. We knew the Goushchins must be watching us and reporting back to their Embassy. We waited. Nothing happened. Our blissful life went on.

In May, Galina flew to Moscow to take her scheduled annual leave. I wasn't at all happy to see her go. I didn't say anything, but I felt quite sick with fear that she might never come back.

Her old friend L and his wife were on the same flight. I knew Galina was very concerned about them, because the marriage was going through a sticky patch. L's wife had got a bit too fond of partying around Lusaka, and not always with her husband.

I said, 'Better not get too involved. It's their business.'

10

Moscow: May 1976

Galina had orders to report to Antonina Nicolayevna at the Ministry of Education as soon as she got back to Moscow.

'You've had a bad time,' Antonina Nicolayevna said with a sympathetic smile. 'We think it will be best for you to stay here in Moscow. Maybe Africa is not good for you.'

Galina began to protest, but the other woman cut her off. 'Don't worry, it won't affect your record. We'll simply cancel the rest of your contract on medical grounds. Report to the clinic in one week's time.'

They must know about Peter! The Goushchins must have told the Embassy she was living with him, breaking the rules. She had known all along that something like this would happen. If she didn't pass the medical, the Ministry would make her stay in Moscow. She would never see Peter again.

The doctors at the clinic found nothing wrong with her. They put her through a rigorous medical examination but could find no reason to refuse her a certificate of fitness.

Clutching the precious certificate, Galina went straight to the Ministry. If Antonina Nicolayevna tried to keep her in Moscow now, she would have to think of another reason. But Antonina Nicolayevna seemed pleased that the doctors had pronounced Galina fit. All she said was, 'That's fine. You can go back to Zambia, if that's what you want.'

'Yes, it's what I want. I enjoy teaching there.' And everything else, she thought, smiling innocently at her superior.

Antonina Nicolayevna moved away to the window of her office. With her back to Galina she said, 'How would you like it if we arranged a move to Lusaka for you? Your prospects for promotion would be much better there. I believe you could do very well. It would be an excellent career move.' She turned around. 'What do you say?'

Galina thought fast. Lusaka would be better than Moscow, but she would still be too far from Peter. 'I would prefer to return to Senanga if that is possible,' she said. 'My work there is on the verge of showing positive results. The Africans are reading our literature and asking questions about Russia. They are talking to me and beginning to trust me. Much ground could be lost if I don't go back to finish the job.'

Whether it was her argument that did the trick, or the visits to the *Beryozka* shop, Galina couldn't be sure, but Antonina Nicolayevna agreed to let her come back to Senanga.

She flew into Africa via Entebbe Airport in Uganda, landing there on 5 July, one day after the dramatic raid when the Israelis saved more than 100 hostages from pro-Palestinian skyjackers. We heard about the rescue on the radio, and I can't tell you how relieved I was when Galina arrived back safely in Senanga.

We settled down into our idyllic life together. How easy it was to live for the day, to live as the Zambians lived, like children for whom tomorrow is a long way away. The only cloud on our horizon was the inescapable fact that my own contract would run out in December.

The Christmas holidays came and I had to leave for the UK, not knowing when or even whether I would be coming back to Zambia. Access to Senanga was still restricted, and it would be impossible to come back without a valid contract.

Since I'd been working in Zambia, Christmas in the UK had always been a special time for me, a time to renew old friendships as well as visiting my parents and grandparents and my brother and his family.

This year was different. Although I went on the usual round

of visits and parties, my heart wasn't in it. All I could think about was how to get another contract signed up so I could get back to Galina. We had grown very close in the months we had been together, and I had accepted and enjoyed our relationship without thinking very much about where it might be heading.

Now we were continents apart I missed Galina desperately. The thought of never seeing her again was, quite simply, unbearable. I needed her in my life.

I spent the whole of January pestering everybody I knew who had contacts with the Zambians, pleading for help to get a new teaching contract in Senanga. Persistence paid off, and at the end of the month I left Heathrow on a flight to Lusaka.

11

Galina was waiting in our house in Senanga, and I had never known a sweeter homecoming. We threw our arms round each other and danced around the room, laughing and crying all at the same time.

'We'll get married,' I said. 'We'll get married and live happily ever after.'

Galina said nothing. I stopped whirling her around and looked down at her face.

'Galina – darling Galina, you will marry me, won't you?'

But still she said nothing. Her eyes were bright with tears. I saw the sadness on her face and felt the laughter dying in my heart.

'What's wrong? You do love me, don't you? You said you loved me before I went away. You haven't changed your mind, have you?' I felt as cold as ice.

She shook her head. 'No,' she said. 'I haven't changed my mind. I do love you, Peter. But I don't think we can get married. I don't think it will be allowed. I am breaking all the rules, just living with you. That's bad enough. But marriage . . .'

'No!' I heard my own voice shouting. '*No!* I won't let anybody stop us! How could they? Why should they?' I paced around the room, fists clenched, ready to punch any and every Russian who dared try to pull us apart.

'Please,' Galina said. 'please let's not talk about it now. Can't we just enjoy being together again?'

I tried to calm down. Eventually we sat down to eat the meal Galina had prepared to welcome me home.

When we made love that night, it was with a passion more intense than I had ever known, a passion heightened by an edge of danger. Who could know what might lie ahead of us?

All my life, when I wanted something I always went flat out to get it. I never gave up on anything, ever. I wasn't about to start quitting now. I was absolutely determined to marry Galina. Absolutely. Whatever it took. Somehow I would talk her out of her doubts. I had to. Without her, there would be no life worth living.

The term passed and the Easter holidays came round. By this time, Galina had very reluctantly agreed to let me make some discreet enquiries. At least I could find out what obstacles we might have to face.

It had taken a lot of persuasion to get her to this point, and she was still very nervous about the whole enterprise. Oh, for a special licence and a quiet Register Office. Or even Gretna Green and an anvil. How much simpler everything was at home.

We soon learned that a local wedding was out of the question. It couldn't be done without Galina's documents, and the Russian Embassy held her passport and all her papers. She told me flatly that under no circumstances did she want her Embassy to know anything about our plans. If she asked for her papers, the Russians would certainly demand to know what she wanted them for.

Without Galina's papers we could do nothing.

12

Zambia: April 1977

We were getting nowhere. The thought was beginning to haunt
me that it might prove just too difficult for us to get married.
Perhaps I understood the problems now even better than
Galina did.

We considered the pros and cons of throwing ourselves on
the mercy of the Zambian authorities and pleading for special
dispensation, but that was an option we dismissed pretty fast.
We had to be realistic. For what possible reason would the
Zambians protect a pair of silly lovers and risk the embarrassment of upsetting the Russians?

The more I thought about it, the more marriage began to
look impossible. But I was still determined to try. We decided
we would have our honeymoon first and deal with the formalities later.

We left Senanga with our Scottish friends Graham and Sarah
Smith, and set off for Luansha, a town in the Copper Belt. A
friend of Graham and Sarah's had generously invited us all to
stay in his private house.

We were rather taken aback when, immediately after greeting us, our host suggested we chain our cars to a large tree in
the yard. Theft was rife, he explained, not so much from
Zambians as from raiders who came in from neighbouring
Zaire. These bandits would cross the border, snatch cars, and
disappear into the night.

First thing in the morning, I told our host that robbers had taken his tree as well as the cars. He got to the window before he realized I was joking.

We stayed in the Copper Belt for a couple of days, and introduced Galina to the delights of Chinese food. Chinese cuisine is one of my favourites, and Galina had never tasted it before. She loved it all. She took such pleasure in sampling barbecued spare ribs, king prawns in sweet and sour sauce, saffron rice, crispy noodles, lychees in syrup . . . a glass of red wine, a glass of white . . . she was like a child at her first party.

Her expressions of wonder at the vast choice on the menu and the quantity and variety of food that arrived at our table brought back a memory from my childhood. I remembered an elderly man, the father of a Czech friend of a family living next door. He came to England in the late 1950s, I think it was, on a visit from Czechoslovakia. The families went out in a party to a restaurant, and though I can't recall his name, I've always remembered the look on his face when he saw the spread of food on the table, the good wines, the Havana cigar he was given.

'So many things, so many wonderful things.' I remembered how he sat there fighting back tears. 'So many wonderful things – and all at the same time . . .'

Galina's expression was just like that old father's. So many wonderful things . . . and all at the same time. After Moscow, this must seem like a fairy tale.

The next day, on impulse, we left Graham and Sarah in Luansha and drove through Lusaka to Livingstone. The journey was long, more than 500 miles, but the road was reasonable and we made good time.

In Livingstone, we booked into the Rainbow Lodge on Victoria Falls Road, right at the side of the Falls. We had our own private *rondavel*, a kind of superior grass hut with a wooden floor and simple furnishings. We had all the service we would have had in the main hotel building, but the blessing of peace and privacy whenever we wanted it. Which was most of the time.

This was a very special time for us, and the last thing we

wanted was the company of other expats or tourists. This was our honeymoon. I tried not to worry that we might never have a real one.

I had been looking forward to watching Galina's face when she first set eyes on the Falls. She didn't disappoint me. Her delight was everything I hoped for and more.

Here at the Victoria Falls the sleepy-looking Zambezi we knew at Senanga turns a corner and changes into what the Zambians call *mosi au tunya*, 'the smoke that thunders'. We watched the white hissing water crashing at 575 tons a second into the Batoka Gorge nearly 100 feet below. The warm spray drenched us in minutes. We laughed and danced about and flicked water at each other's faces like children, as if we hadn't a worry in the world.

I had seen so many marvellous places in Africa, from Uganda to the Cape, and I wanted to show them all to Galina.

Those days in our private paradise made me even more determined to hold on to this wonder, this ever deepening love that Galina and I had found together. Somehow, somewhere, we *would* get married.

Our holiday was almost over, and soon we would have to go back to Senanga and the daily routine of school. The rainy season was coming to an end and, if we could get to Mongu at exactly the right time, our 'honeymoon' would finish with a spectacle we would both remember for the rest of our lives.

I wanted Galina beside me to watch the Lozi ceremony of the Kuomboka. This was an experience I had enjoyed very much when I first came to Zambia. It was something very special, and I wanted us to share it.

Before we headed back to Mongu, we stopped over for a couple of nights in Lusaka, where we were scheduled to meet a Welsh friend of mine, Brian Nelson. We wanted to be there to give him whatever comfort and support we could when he said goodbye to his wife, Rosalind, and their children, who were travelling home to Wales. It was quite usual for an expatriate wife to go home before her husband, to sort out housing and schools in the UK, while the husband stayed on for maybe a year to earn more money for the family.

We joined Brian and his family for a farewell lunch, then we all trooped out to the airport with everybody doing their best to be cheerful. I was following the others through the airport lounge when a man suddenly approached me and said, 'Excuse me, but do you have the right time?'

This struck me as a very odd thing to ask. There was a huge great clock on the wall, and the London flight had just been called. Then I noticed his tie.

'Nice tie,' I said.

'Yes, it's from the High Commission.'

I knew it was, and made a quick decision. I said, 'I want to come in to discuss something with you.'

'Yes, I thought you might. We know all about you. We wondered when you'd be coming in to Lusaka.'

'I'll be in tomorrow.'

We saw Brian's family off, and had a farewell drink with him. We promised to come and see him soon at his house in Mongu. Then, as the three of us headed in the direction of the car park, Galina gripped my arm. She pulled me back so we fell a few paces behind Brian.

'Don't look round,' she whispered, 'but I think there is a man over there who is KGB. About twenty yards away, to your left.'

We kept walking. Peering out of the corner of my eye and trying not to turn my head, I saw a man who seemed to be roaming about to no particular purpose.

If Galina was right, what was he doing here? We knew there was no flight either to or from Moscow at this time. Earlier, while we were waiting for Brian, Galina had wandered over to look at a flight information board. The next plane to Moscow wasn't due to fly out till the day after tomorrow.

I didn't want to burden Brian with our problems. After all, his family had only just gone and he must be feeling pretty low himself. It didn't occur to me till after we'd waved him off that our problems might have helped take his mind off his troubles. He might also have had some ideas to offer.

Galina and I were due at the Longacres Hotel in Lusaka, a teachers' hostel where we had arranged to meet one of my best friends, Kaye Townsend, who was Head of the International School in Lusaka. Kaye had once been Head at Senanga, long before my time there, and Galina and I used to pitch down with him whenever we were in Lusaka.

As we drove towards the hostel I thought and thought about the implications of what had just happened. The skin at the back of my neck was tingling. Who had told the British I was involved with a Russian? Why was a Russian agent lurking around the airport when a British plane was flying out? The tingle spread down my spine. Were they watching Galina? Or me? Or both of us?

Kaye was waiting for us in the bar. We made some small talk, but I couldn't get the men at the airport out of my head. I couldn't stop myself pouring out the whole story.

'Nothing else for it, old man,' Kaye said at the end of the saga. 'You're going to have to go to the British High Commission, see what they advise.'

I'd more than half expected he would say that.

Kaye looked at Galina, then at me. He said, 'It looks pretty obvious to me you can't carry on like this. It'll wear you down – or tear you apart.'

13

Zambia: April 1977

Overnight I did some hard thinking. In the morning, I took Galina with me to the British High Commission. There was no sign of the man who had asked me the time at the airport.

The two High Commission officials we saw were very courteous and listened carefully as we explained our dilemma. Both men shook their heads. 'We can only handle the lady's business if she asks for political asylum. We can't deal with the Russians directly. Afraid you'll have to go to the Russian Embassy yourselves. Sorry, old man, nothing we can do.'

Galina felt she was caught between the proverbial rock and a hard place. She wanted very much for us to get married, but she didn't want to jeopardize her chances of going back to Moscow. If she asked for political asylum, she might never see her mother again.

Besides, she was still very pro-Russian. She didn't think her country was any worse than others, and she still believed strongly in the ideology her whole life had been built around. She didn't want to let down her family and her friends.

She agonized aloud as we walked along Independence Avenue. She didn't believe the Russians would do anything to damage her romance. Why should they bother? She wasn't important enough. Anyway, Russia had signed the Helsinki Agreement in 1975, hadn't she? The agreement included the right for Russian citizens to marry foreigners, didn't it? Of course her country would honour its commitment.

'And I don't think it's decent to ask for political asylum. I couldn't do that, it would be too big a step to take. It would be an insult to my country,' she said.

I remembered how this country she was so determined not to insult had left her lying for weeks in a foreign hospital, without so much as a visit from her own people. I said nothing. This was no time for cruel reminders. But we would have to think very hard about what to do next.

We had a bite of lunch, though neither of us felt much like eating. Then we went for a drive to the botanical gardens at Munda Wanga, some 20 miles down the road that went through Kafue Township and on to Livingstone in the south.

We were strolling in the gardens when I caught sight of a man I thought looked very like the Russian Galina had pointed out at the airport. Come on, Peter, I said to myself, you're getting paranoid. I said nothing to Galina.

But it wasn't paranoia. A few minutes later Galina noticed him too, so we gradually edged closer. There was no doubt about it, it really was the same man. The Russians had followed us to this remote beauty spot. A little too much of a coincidence, I thought.

We headed off west, determined not to spoil the last days of our holiday by worrying. We had better things to do.

Our timing was spot-on. It was nearly the full moon, the rainy season was ending, and the Zambezi was beginning to overflow into the flood plains of Barotseland. And the next day was a Thursday, as tradition required.

The Litunga, the king of the Lozi people, chooses this precise time to leave his lowland palace at Lealui to travel to his second palace at Limulunga. There he takes up residence on the high ground above the flood plain.

The Kuomboka ceremony always attracts a lot of local attention. Some years ago Armand and Michaela Denis made a film of the ceremony, but as the country didn't have television at that time very few Zambians knew it had been seen by the outside world.

Early in the morning we went down to the river and took a motor boat. This was the only means of getting to the palace, which now stood in splendid isolation on an island created by the floodwater on the Barotse plain. The procession would take most of the day before it reached its climax in the ceremonial disembarkation. I gave Galina no hint about what would happen there, so as not to spoil the surprise.

We watched in fascination, holding hands like a couple of teenagers, as three huge drums were brought into the palace courtyard. We saw the Litunga himself come out to start off the drumming, then the royal drummers took over. They would keep up the steady beat till the drums were taken on board the royal barge, the *Nalikwanda*, to accompany the king on his journey.

'But these drums – they're enormous!'

'They certainly are. They're over a metre wide and stand a metre high,' I said, delighted to show off my knowledge. 'They're about a hundred and fifty years old. They've even got names.'

'I'm not sure whether I think that's wonderful – or just silly,' Galina said. 'Why should drums have names? Do you know what the names are?'

Of course I knew. This expedition was intended to give us both a day to remember, but it was also a chance for me to impress Galina. I'd done my homework well in advance.

'They're called "*Kanaona*", "*Munanga*", and "*Mundili*". The drumbeats are meant to travel over the floodwater to let the whole of the Litunga's kingdom know he's setting off on his journey to his palace on the high ground.'

'And the boat – what did you call it?'

'The *Nalikwanda*.'

Galina rolled the name around her tongue. '*Na-lik-wan-da*. It looks like a great big canoe.'

'You're right – it is a canoe, and it's made of wood. It was made by a German carpenter around the beginning of the century, and it takes a hundred men to paddle it.'

'A hundred! That many?'

'Yes, and if any paddler isn't mucking in, he gets chucked overboard.'

82

The Litunga would ask for certain boys from our school, usually close relatives of his, to row the barge for him. Galina hadn't known about this, and she began to scan the paddlers' faces to see if she could recognize any of our boys.

I said, 'It's a great honour to be chosen to paddle the royal barge, so nobody wants the disgrace of being ditched in the floodwater. Imagine the shame if you had to swim ashore in front of all these people.'

The *Nalikwanda* is painted with broad black-and-white stripes, and the Litunga sits enthroned beneath a half-dome of canvas and reeds which protects him from the sun. A black elephant made from papier mâché is mounted on top of this dome, and above the elephant the Litunga's personal flag flies, the black silhouette of an elephant on a brilliant red ground. All through the journey the royal orchestra proclaims the king's progress with drums and xylophones.

'Look,' I pointed. 'There's another boat coming up behind. That's the queen's boat.'

The queen's barge is as splendid as the king's, but not quite so large. Behind it a flotilla of vessels carries the royal couple's servants and attendants, with local dignitaries and people of the tribe, who come in from townships and villages all over the Western Province.

'What are those boats doing in front of the Litunga's canoe?' Galina was pointing to the head of the procession where three dugouts were leading the way.

'They're making sure there's a channel that's deep enough for the Litunga's boat. It would never do for him to get stuck in the shallows.'

We watched the royal procession and listened to the drums till the boats were no more than specks on the horizon. Then we took our boat back to Mongu, where we picked up some cooked chicken and mangoes and beer. We found an ideal spot by the river with trees to protect us from the sun. We put up a makeshift canvas shelter and ate our picnic and drank warm beer, and on this magical day they tasted like ambrosia and nectar from the gods.

We collected the car and drove the 12 miles upriver to

Limulunga, where we waited for the flotilla. As the Litunga's barge came into sight a troupe of women in traditional dress began to dance on the shore, making a great show of enticing him to step off his boat and come ashore among them.

Galina gasped in amazement when she saw the king. He had changed his clothes, and very splendid he looked, too. He was dressed in the full uniform of a British admiral, gold-braided jacket, ostrich-plumed hat, the works. According to tradition, when each Litunga comes to the throne he has this wonderful outfit tailored for him in London.

'Unbelievable,' Galina said when I explained this. Then she covered her mouth to hush a sudden chuckle. Between her fingers, so no one else could hear, she laughed, 'Does he keep his feathers cool along with his drinks?'

I knew what she meant. I had thought it pretty funny myself, the first time I saw it. In the stern of the royal canoe stood a gleaming white refrigerator. I thought about the warm beer we had drunk with our picnic. Tradition be blowed, the Litunga got full marks for practicality.

The Kuomboka ceremony ends when the Litunga is escorted into his palace. Then the whole of Barotseland enjoys an orgy of feasting and celebration which can easily last the rest of the week.

For us, though, this very special day was over. Our 'honeymoon' was almost over, too. We headed straight off so we could drive in daylight, and all the way to Senanga we talked about the precious memories we were taking with us.

So we travelled back to real life, still without a clue about what we should do next. Whatever we did, we'd have to be extremely careful. I had read about cases where Russians were condemned to 25 years in a penal colony for having an affair with a foreigner. And not so very long ago, either. The more I thought about the whole business, the more convinced I became that Galina could be in real danger.

I wasn't far wrong.

14

Mongu, Zambia: May 1977

First thing next morning, Galina was summoned to the school office. The headmaster, Mr Mukela, didn't beat about the bush.

'You are on immediate transfer to Mongu, Miss Vasilyeva. There is a flat waiting for you. It has been decided that you should work out your contract in Mongu.'

'But why? I don't understand . . .'

The gentle Zambian's eyes were sad. He shook his head. 'Come, my dear lady, I'm sure you do understand. It's in everybody's best interest that you leave Senanga before the new term begins . . . for your own sake, but especially for the sake of the pupils' moral well-being. The Education Authority has taken the decision.'

He offered her a handshake. 'You are not being sacked, only transferred. It could have been worse.'

Galina caught the next local bus to Mongu to try to sort out this unexpected problem. The official she saw at the Education Authority offered to 'fix everything' so she could stay in Senanga . . . all she had to do was grant him a few personal favours. Galina held on to her temper long enough to turn down the offer with civility, but she was seething with anger and distress all the way back to Senanga.

The very next day, this official arrived by plane at our tiny airstrip and came straight to Galina's house. From his cocksure manner, he was confident she would think better of her refusal.

'You were very insistent you wanted to stay on here in Senanga,' he reminded her. 'I have a lot of influence. Maybe you should think a little more about my offer.'

Galina felt like pushing the fellow bodily out of the house, but managed to stifle the urge. She made him a cup of coffee instead.

I had gone down with some kind of fever and was lying in the darkened bedroom feeling sorry for myself when Galina answered this man's knock at her door. My illness had settled on my chest and I was racked with constant coughing. Only one door separated the bedroom from the sitting-room, and all the time he sat there chatting up Galina and drinking our coffee I had to lie there with a sufficating blanket pressed to my face, trying not to make a sound. If this official found out I was actually living in Galina's house it could wreck our chances of ever getting permission to marry.

Galina eventually got rid of the man, but she didn't manage to stay in Senanga. There were bigger fish than him trying to separate us.

Galina spent a few more days in Senanga with no job, waiting for her new school's Land Rover to fetch her back to Mongu. I helped her pack the basics she would need, and when her lift arrived we said a very tearful goodbye.

It was some small consolation that she would be in Mongu, where I had friends. Visits would still be possible, so things were not too serious yet. But they were far from good.

I was very unhappy and very lonely, and when the chance came a few weeks later to see Galina I was over the moon. I had to travel to Lusaka on school business, and drove to Galina's flat on the way, praying she would be there. Her flat was close to Brian Nelson's house, so if by some mischance Galina was not at home, I could call in on Brian.

Imagine my feelings when my knock on her door was answered by a man ... a man wearing nothing but a pair of briefs. He made a bad-tempered gesture and growled, 'What do you want?'

'Galina Vasilyeva? Isn't this her place?'

'Galina? She's here, but she's in bed.'

The accent was thick, but not so thick I couldn't understand what the man was saying. She's in bed ... my Galina ... and here's this gorilla with next to nothing on ... I rushed out of the building, jumped into my car and drove the 400 miles to Lusaka half-blind with rage.

I felt desperately alone travelling down those hundreds of miles on my own. There was no one to share my feelings with, no one to commiserate with me.

This was the woman I was going to marry ... all those tears when she left me in Senanga ... what kind of woman was she? What did I actually know about her? How could she do this to me? I hated her. I loved her. What on earth was I going to do?

When eventually I pulled up at the Lusaka Hotel I was shaking with exhaustion and jealousy. Oh yes, this was one outraged expat feeling desperately sorry for himself. And wishing he'd given that fellow a punch on the nose, at the very least.

My good friend Brian drove all the way along that same road to Lusaka the next day, to find me and tell me the real story. If I hadn't gone off in such a huff, he said, I could have found out for myself what had actually happened.

A Yugoslav company had come to Mongu to do some work for the water department, and as Galina was living on her own in a government flat a Yugoslav couple had been billeted with her.

When Galina first went to live in the flat she found it absolutely filthy. Everything was thick with grease and grime, and it looked as if nothing had been cleaned for years. She worked day and night cleaning it, trying to make it habitable before she started at her new school. Once she started teaching she wouldn't have the time for so much heavy domestic work. Whether she had caught some infection from the dirt in the flat or had simply picked up a bug somewhere she couldn't tell, but she suddenly became very ill.

I was conscience-stricken, remembering how ill I had been

during our last days together in Senanga. Had I passed something on to her?

Apparently these Yugoslavs had taken over the flat and treated it as if it was their own, while Galina was feeling too awful to protest.

After I had jumped to all the wrong conclusions and steamed off in a rage, Galina asked, 'Who was at the door?' When her 'lodger' answered, 'Some English, big fellow with a beard – told him you're in bed and he went away,' she guessed what had happened. Maybe she knew me better than I knew myself.

I felt thoroughly ashamed of all the terrible things I had been thinking about Galina, my prime concern now was to make sure she was all right.

My business in Lusaka kept me there for almost a week. As soon as she was well enough, Galina braved the bone-shaking bus journey to come to the capital to see me. Feeling even worse, now I'd had time to brood about my behaviour, I confessed my terrible jealousy and my distress that we had nearly lost each other because of my huge silly mistake.

We had to do something to resolve the situation. We couldn't let this stress go on. Sooner or later something would happen that might not be so easy to forgive. We must write to the Russian authorities.

'I can't do it, I can't write,' Galina said. 'It will be a document. It's not allowed. It will be another mark on my record.' But write she did. There was nothing else left to do.

'I, Galina Vasilyeva, wish to get married to an Englishman, Mr Peter Young, and I ask your permission to do so. Yours sincerely etc.'

The Russian Embassy in Lusaka was not an encouraging place. I rang the bell outside a door set in high iron gates, and a disembodied Dalek voice asked me what my business was. To deliver a letter, I said.

The door gave a loud click. I went in. The door clanged shut behind me and another loud click let me know it had locked. This did not fill me with confidence.

I found myself in a large yard crammed with trucks. I had often seen trucks like these, with their 'TZ' registration plates, going in and out of the Embassy grounds. Everybody knew they belonged to the freedom fighters who were fighting against Ian Smith's white regime in Rhodesia. I crossed the yard to the main door of the building. Another door, another wait till this door, too, opened to let me enter.

My experience of Russian officials was precisely nil. The man waiting behind the reception desk could not have been more polite or more helpful, the very model of diplomatic correctness in his neat dark suit.

His colleague, a man sitting to one side behind him, gave me what I took to be an encouraging nod. I handed over the letter. The official read it. Not a muscle of his face moved. He looked straight at me. To my profound relief, he smiled.

We talked about the matter in some detail. The discussion was conducted in friendly tones, but there was no chair on my side of the desk, and the Russian remained standing, too.

I was very keyed up all the while, and very much aware of being in Russian territory, totally at the mercy of the Embassy. No one knew I was here except Galina, a Russian. In such a situation, your imagination runs wild . . . they could refuse to let you leave . . . you could disappear without trace. Here in their own Embassy, the Russians could do anything they liked. It was quite scary.

The official was very affable, very encouraging. 'No problem,' he said. 'No problem at all.'

His colleague sauntered over to join him and they seemed relaxed, almost jolly, as they quoted the Helsinki agreement. They had, they said, the greatest respect for its stand on human rights. Marriages between Russians and foreigners are allowed, no problem, just leave the letter.

I felt almost optimistic as I drove Galina back to Mongu. It looked as if everything might, just might, be okay. She blew kisses from the doorway of her building as I drove off past Brian's house and headed for the road to Senanga.

*

89

Just before lunch the next day, a search party arrived to summon me to the airstrip beside the school compound. Frank, the headmaster at Galina's school in Mongu, wanted to see me. His plane had a short stop in transit – I should dash over to the airstrip at once.

Dash I did, and Frank wasted no time. 'Did you know the Russians are coming to take Galina Vasilyeva back to Moscow?'

He knew down to the last detail what was going on. As head of the school, he had to be informed of the imminent arrival of the Russian delegation. Everyone in Mongu knew what was happening.

Galina had received a telegram that morning saying her mother was dying and needed her at home straight away. The Embassy was sending a car to pick her up, and would get her back to Moscow with all possible speed. The Embassy had given the other Russians in the Kambule school compound the whole story. They had orders to keep Galina in the dark and to make a big show of sympathizing with her.

These Russians were a married couple who had a reputation for making themselves very helpful to everybody. The husband, Vitaly, also broke the rules by making friends with the English teachers and socializing openly with them. He appeared very Westernized compared with other Russians in the region, and even possessed a car he had somehow negotiated from other expatriates. You could say he was a capitalist by nature, if not by religion.

However, the instant he got this message from his Embassy he reverted to being the model Communist, directing all his efforts to keeping up the charade that Galina's mother was ill.

As Galina's headmaster, Frank had been asked to give her compassionate leave for a month. Frank was a South African Coloured who had taught with me in Kaoma, and we had been the best of friends throughout that time. I owed him a great debt for taking the trouble to tell me what was happening.

'I'll go to Mongu tomorrow, as soon as I've —'

'No!' The interruption was explosive. 'Today! You must go

90

today. You must go *now*. Tomorrow will be too late. She'll be gone before you get there.'

I ran to Myra's and told her what was happening. 'I'll bring Galina back here. We'll have to hide her. We can't let the Russians take her – I might never see her again.'

15

Mongu, Zambia: May 1977

I drove the dirt road to Mongu like a maniac. This calamity was all my fault. I had disregarded my own fears as well as Galina's, now God alone knew what price she might have to pay if they got her back to Moscow.

The rainy season was barely over, and the road was still a quagmire. The Datsun bumped, lurched, groaned, splashed, mile after desperate mile. Halfway to Mongu I rattled up to a man standing on the road beside his Land Rover, the vehicle axle-deep in mud and sand. I knew this notorious black spot well. Many a time I'd helped dig out cars, Land Rovers, even buses.

For the first time in all my years in Africa I didn't stop. It was an unwritten rule of the road that if you came across a driver in trouble you stopped and helped. I'd been on the receiving end of assistance many times myself, and I felt pretty rotten now. But I felt even worse about Galina. I kept going.

'You'll never get a car through this,' the man shouted after me.

'Watch me!' I yelled back, and carried on at breakneck speed.

In Africa there's a saying that no one but a drunk drives straight up the middle of the road – the only way to drive is to weave from side to side dodging the bumps and holes. There are ways and means of getting through this kind of terrain, and I had perfected most of them. Even so, I was relieved and more than a little amazed to arrive in Mongu with no damage to myself and nothing worse than a few scratches and dents to the Datsun.

Already, two Russians were there in Galina's flat, a couple of real heavies. My experience of the Russian heavy mob was limited to a passing acquaintance with *The Man From Uncle* on TV. They were nothing like the dapper Ilya Kuryakin, these gorillas. I'm a big man, but they were bigger. A lot bigger. In Galina's own words, this is what happened:

'Russians seldom came to Mongu. Before they came, my colleague Vitaly was trying to persuade me that everything would be all right. They had told him to keep me quiet while the arrangements were made. Till then I thought he was on my side, always sympathetic about Peter, always telling me things would work out.

'Then the Russian Embassy car came, and the Colonel of the KGB got out. This was the man I had already met when I came first to Lusaka, the man my friend L told me was KGB. He was followed by two men. When these men stood up I saw they were absolutely huge.

'They said they came on trade business, and of course they brought vodka. They also brought a telegram. It said my mother was dying and the doctors were demanding my immediate presence at the hospital.

'You see something like this, and you know you don't really believe it, but still you think it might be true.

'I still believed in the system at this time. I saw a telegram written by doctors and endorsed by the Embassy. It was possible my mother was very ill, how could I say for sure if it was true or not?

'I am thinking how I am her only daughter and there are no other close relatives. I would never forgive myself if my mother died all alone. I just didn't know what to do.

'The man from the KGB says, "We will sign our trade agreement tomorrow morning, then we'll go straight back to Lusaka. We can give you a lift, it will all go very nicely."

'I say no, I have to see Peter before I go. I left the building and ran like crazy around Mongu, asking if anybody was going to Senanga, if anybody could give me a lift. Nobody tried to stop me doing this. But there were no lifts, nobody going to Senanga that day. The soonest lift would be in two or three days.

'I went back to my flat and told the delegation no, I would not go with them the next day. I was playing for time, trying to hold on for just a little longer. Trying to think of a way to get a message to Peter.

'All the members of the delegation were so sympathetic. It was play-acting at its best. "No, no," they said. "We are scheduled to leave tomorrow. We cannot wait any longer."

'By the greatest of good fortune, my headmaster, Frank, had reached Peter and told him the story. Peter came that same evening, the evening before we were supposed to go.

'These Russians were staying in my flat. When Peter arrived they met him like a long-lost brother. They drank vodka with him. They ate a meal with us, and they drank more vodka. They said they would stay overnight in my flat, and we would leave in the morning.'

When I got to Galina's place, these fellows acted like big amiable teddy bears, as nice as could be.

'Don't worry, don't worry at all,' they said. 'She's only going home for a little while. Her mother is very ill. She has to see her mother. The doctors say it will help. She'll be back in a month. Look, she's leaving all her stuff here. Don't worry at all.'

They smiled and spread their arms wide in a gesture apparently meant to reassure us. 'We've come all the way out here because we're very concerned about her. We're taking her back so she can see her mother before something serious happens . . .'

The friendly persuasion went on and on. I didn't believe a word of it. I said to Galina, 'Don't believe this. It's nonsense. It's all lies, they're telling you lies. Come back with me. We'll look after you, everybody will help us. For God's sake, listen to me! Don't go!'

The Russians showed no reaction to this outburst. Their smiles got even wider and they turned up the charm. 'We're staying here in Galina Vasilyeva's flat tonight,' they said.

'Would you like to stay with her tonight? You know, as if nothing has happened? We're sorry she has to go. Please stay here with her tonight.'

I said no. My friend Brian Nelson's house was right across the street. That's where I planned to stay, and Galina was coming with me. The Russians would have to use force to stop us, and I was taking a gamble they wouldn't do that. They wouldn't want any fuss. They might watch Brian's house all night, they might watch my car in case we slipped away into the dark, but I didn't care.

We would spend the rest of the evening with Brian, and then have the night together in private. Brian would be happy to put us up, now he was on his own while his wife was back in the UK. He'd be glad of some company for a few hours.

The Russians let us go without protest. They didn't even suggest putting a guard on us.

I tried for hours to convince Galina not to go. I pleaded with her, 'Please don't take any notice of them. They're telling you a pack of lies. There's no trade mission, believe me. They've come out here with the sole purpose of picking you up and taking you back to Moscow so you won't get married to a Westerner. They'll take you to Moscow, and you'll never come back again.'

But Galina only kept on saying over and over again, 'I must go back with them. I don't know whether my mother is ill or not, but I must go to see her in case it's true. There's nothing else I can do.'

So we spent our last night in Mongu together, and in the morning we hugged each other and said our private goodbyes. Then we left Brian's house to meet Galina's guards – I couldn't think of these goons as anything else.

Galina asked about her things, what should she do about her belongings? She knew her flat was sure to be used while she was away.

'Don't worry, everything will be safe, that's a promise. Leave your things where they are. You'll be back in two or three weeks, a month at the most.'

So Galina left the flat and all her possessions. She got into the car with her Russian minders, and as they drew away from the house she wound down the window and called to me, 'I'll see you in a month.' I could only pray she was right.

The Russians drove Galina to the Embassy in Lusaka, where she was treated very kindly and given her 'stopover allowance', a small amount of local currency for any small items she might want to buy for her journey. Everything was done that could be done to keep up the fiction that this was a routine leave on compassionate grounds.

She wanted to talk to Kaye Townsend. She knew Kaye had grown very fond of her since she and I had been together, and she desperately wanted his advice. Her KGB escort went with her to the house, but Kaye was not there. Then the KGB man left her to sleep in the house of a Russian family she knew. These people never let her out of their sight that night.

On the face of it, all the Russians in Lusaka sympathized with Galina's plight. Long afterwards, she learned that every Russian she came into contact with on her journey, from Lusaka through Dar-es-Salaam to Moscow, had been briefed about her and ordered to confirm the story she had been told.

The next day, Galina's minders drove her to the airport. Her guards took her passport and boarding pass, and while she spent her few kwachas on souvenirs they pocketed her duty-free allowance in vodka and cigarettes.

They put her on a plane to Tanzania. The two seats in front and the two seats behind were reserved, and were swiftly occupied by Russians. It didn't take a genius to work out why they were there.

A married couple 'looked after' her in their house in Dar-es-Salaam. These people told Galina nothing at the time, but later, in Moscow, the wife confided to her that they had orders to keep her happy but to make sure she was never left alone. They were told she was trying to escape to the West.

At Dar-es-Salaam airport, she was escorted on to an Aeroflot plane bound for Moscow. She sat alone, with nothing but a small holdall and the clothes she was wearing. Once again, Russian agents occupied the seats in front and behind. No one spoke to her. She felt she was being treated like a criminal.

All through the long dreary flight she worried and wondered whether she had been told the truth. Her mother was elderly, and had become quite fragile over the last few years. She had a few health problems, Galina knew, but the Russians had refused to give any details about why exactly her mother was in hospital.

Waiting on the runway at Sheremetyevo Airport was Antonina Nicolayevna from the Ministry of Education. She escorted Galina home in a taxi, saw her into her flat, and turned to go.

Galina asked, 'Where is my mother?'

She was half expecting the answer. 'Don't be stupid. There's nothing wrong with your mother. I'll see you tomorrow at the Ministry. We'll make sure you never go abroad again. Never.'

16

The next day, Galina reported to the Ministry. She was told immediately that her contract was cancelled because of her disgraceful behaviour. She would never be permitted to go back to Zambia.

She was given a strong reprimand by the Party, and sharply reminded of the pledge she had signed. She had sworn she would never associate with foreigners and would behave at all times in an appropriate and moral fashion. She had failed in every respect.

She had committed a deeply offensive act, and had disgraced herself, disgraced her school, disgraced her country. She would be dealt with in a manner appropriate to her misdemeanour. She would be dealt with . . .

As soon as she could get to a phone, Galina rang her mother to make sure she really was all right. Her mother said she had no idea what was happening. There had been a telephone call from the authorities telling her Galina Vasilyeva would be returning to Moscow before her contract ended. That was all she knew.

'Why have you come back early? Are you ill? What has happened?'

Galina decided to tell her mother nothing at this stage. It would be safer for everyone concerned. 'Nothing, really, I'm not ill, it's just a change in the contract arrangements.'

'Oh? You came back just for that? Well, come and see me soon, won't you?' Her mother sounded less than convinced.

The disciplinary procedures began on Monday morning, with an appearance before the Party Central Committee. 30 Party officials, men and women, sat in chairs arranged in a semi-circle. Most of them looked like old Bolsheviks, nearly all in their seventies and eighties.

'Stand in the middle,' someone barked. The Committee conferred, and Galina waited. She looked around the huge room. This must have been some Tsarist prince's palace in the old days. The walls were panelled from floor to ceiling in wood so dark with age she couldn't tell if it was oak, mahogany or rosewood.

She looked up at the ceiling, where sweeps of moulded plaster converged to a flaking gilt rose from which hung an enormous chandelier. Once magnificent, its crystal pendants were grey with dust, and no one had bothered to replace the many spent bulbs. The lights reflected in the cold shiny marble floor, making the seated Committee appear to be floating on its surface.

Galina waited and waited. She began to feel she was shrinking in the vastness of this enormous room, getting smaller and still smaller, no more significant than an ant.

It's a fine art, isn't it, the art of making people feel small. The regime in Galina's Moscow was no different from the Tsarist aristocracy who had built this palace. The wider and higher you made the buildings, the monuments and the statues, the more small and helpless and irrelevant you made people feel. Galina recognized the psychology of power. She must not let it break her.

The questions began suddenly, coming at her like missiles and from different angles so she had to turn her head to look at each questioner. The interrogation was very thorough, like a court hearing but without a court's dignity. Everybody shouted at her.

She was determined not to cry. Absolutely determined. She

would only survive if she played the game their way. Somehow she had to beat the system. She must keep her nerve.

Committee: Why did you deceive your country?

Galina: I didn't

Committee: Why did you go with a foreigner? Don't we have enough men in our country? Are our men not good enough for you?

Galina (laughing): Does it matter?

Committee: He is an Englishman, a capitalist. You wanted to marry a capitalist?

Galina: No, he's just a teacher.

Committee: Who are his parents? What is his family?

Galina: His father is a railway worker. His mother is a secretary.

Derisory laughter ripples round the room.

Committee: You wanted to marry him so you could have money. How rich is he?

Galina: No. He's not rich, he's just an ordinary worker.

Committee: Don't you know he was going to use you because he wanted your secrets?

Galina: What secrets do I have? I only know about school.

Committee: Do you know he is married? We have his file. He is married with two children.

Galina: No.

Committee: But he told you lies.

Galina: No. An Englishman's word is his bond. An English gentleman would not tell lies.

A pause, a lot of muttering, then the questions begin again.

Committee: You said you loved him, right?

Galina: I do. I do love him.

Committee: And you think he loves you?

Galina: I believe he loves me, yes.

Committee: Look at you. What is there to love? Look at yourself. Go and look at yourself in the mirror. What could any man see to love about you? Of course he was using you. Give him up, give him up. We'll give you your job back. We'll even give you promotion. We'll send you to do

100

research work. You are an intelligent woman. We'll give you everything you want. Only give him up.

Galina: Why should I?

Committee: Don't you love your country?

Galina: Yes, I do.

Committee: Then why do you go with a foreigner? You must choose between your work and him.

Galina: I want both. I love my country, and I would do everything I could for Russia. But this is nothing to do with that. He is the man for me, and I love him.

Ever more pointless and repetitive, the questions go on and on. The more the Committee mocks, the stronger Galina feels and the more determined she becomes not to give in. She will never renounce the man she loves. Never.

On Tuesday Galina was summoned to the Ministry, then to the Party's City and District Committees. More questions, more condemnations.

On and on and on. She would not give in. She would not give up Peter.

Her headmistress, her old friend Lydia Ivanovna, was advised of her disgraceful behaviour and ordered not to take her back on her staff. There was nothing she could do. Galina lost her job. What was she to do? She had currency roubles in the bank, but without a salary to live on, these would soon disappear. She had to find work.

She knew of one school where the entire curriculum was taught in English, an English Medium School. With nothing left to lose, she rang the headmistress and asked, 'Do you teach maths in English?'

They did. 'I would like to apply for a post, please.' Galina held her breath. 'Come along and see me.'

Galina went to the school and talked with the headmistress, M, for almost half an hour. M seemed impressed with her qualifications and experience. She sat back in her chair, smiled and said, 'I like you. I'll take you.'

Keeping her voice as steady as she could, Galina told her, 'I have a bad record, a Party reprimand for disgraceful behaviour.'

'What did you do?'

'I want to get married to a foreigner, an Englishman I met in Zambia.'

M thought for a minute, then said, 'Okay, you're here now. Forget him. You'll never see him again. They won't let him come here, and you will never go abroad again, so forget it. But I like you and I like your honesty. I'll take you.'

She smiled again, and went on, 'I can always say, if a good Communist makes a mistake, how can she correct that mistake? Obviously by doing good work.'

So M took Galina on and gave her a job, but just to be on the safe side made her promise that if a miracle should happen and her Englishman somehow managed to come to Moscow, she would quit immediately. Galina promised.

They went to a currency shop.

Almost as soon as Galina started her new job M was summoned to the Ministry of Education. Ministry officials asked her if she was aware of her new staff member's record.

Yes, she said, Galina Vasilyeva had been honest and open about what had happened. M repeated to the officials what she had said to Galina, that she thought it was right that a teacher with such a good previous record should be given a chance to become once again a good Party member.

At school next day she sent for Galina and told her about the interview at the Ministry. 'You can see, can't you, this won't be forgotten. You must make sure you don't do anything, anything at all, to attract attention. The results will be bad for me as well as you.'

M didn't know much about England, but she knew a great deal about Scotland. She was very proud to be a member of the Robert Burns Society, and she visited Scotland every year to celebrate the Scottish poet's anniversary on 25 January. The poetry of 'Rabbie' Burns was very popular in Russia, and had been for many years. To please her benefactor, Galina tried to read some of it, but the charms of the Scots dialect would forever remain a mystery to her.

Galina knew the risks M had taken and she was grateful enough for the employment, but it was not what she really wanted. What she really wanted was to be with her Englishman. Now she must begin to make some very delicate and difficult negotiations. One thought beat a constant drum in her head: 'I want! I want! I want!'

17

Five weeks passed without a word from Galina.

As soon as I could get away from school, I drove to Lusaka and went to the Russian Consulate. I recognised the man at the reception desk. He was a KGB colonel, one of the men who had sat in Galina's flat eating her food and drinking her vodka.

'Galina Vasilyeva – you remember she had to go home to Moscow to see her mother who was ill? Back in May? You came to her flat with her escorts.'

No response.

'We met then. You must remember. We had a drink together.'

Still no response.

I kept my voice even. 'Can you tell me, please, when she will be coming back?'

The man's face remained blank. His eyes revealed nothing, not even curiosity. He said, 'What name did you say? Galina who?'

'Galina Vasilyeva.'

He shook his head, chewed his lip, shook his head again and looked me straight in the eyes. 'Never heard of her.'

'Excuse me?' I said. 'What did you say?'

'Never heard of her.'

I couldn't believe this. 'But I met you in her flat. You *must* remember!'

Another shake of the head, a shrug of the shoulders. Still looking me straight in the eyes he said, 'You must be mistaken.

104

Who is this Galina Vasilyeva? There's never been anyone of that name in Africa. We've never heard of this person.'

My stomach was tying itself in knots. What the hell was going on here?

'But she was in Mongu. She was a teacher here, at Kambule Secondary School. And before that at Senanga.'

'There are only two Russians in Mongu, a married couple. We know nothing about anyone by the name of Galina Vasilyeva.'

As in every African country where Russia had an embassy, mail from Moscow to Zambia came through the diplomatic service in special bags, and was ruthlessly 'sorted'.

Mail from England, however, should have gone straight to Senanga, to Galina, bypassing the Russian Embassy. But ... I remembered how, when I was on holiday in England at Christmas time, I had sent Christmas cards and postcards to Galina and she had never received any of them. Cards addressed to other friends in Zambia were mostly delivered in reasonable time, but not the ones I sent to Galina.

At the time, I put it down to light-fingered Embassy person-nel taking a fancy to postcards from abroad. Maybe someone was building up a collection. Certainly it was annoying, and Galina got a bit upset when she saw my other friends arriving at the bar and passing round Christmas cards 'from England, from Peter', when she hadn't received any herself. I had never read anything sinister into this. Not until now.

The same procedure applied to mail from Africa addressed to the Soviet Union. Everything had to go through the Embassy in Lusaka, and none of my letters were reaching Galina.

I gave letters to friends going out of Zambia on leave, to post from the UK, from France, from Switzerland ... It didn't matter where the letters were sent from, there still no response.

Weeks passed and then months, and still no word came from Galina. I tried to think clearly, to push away the fear that she might have decided to forget me and carry on with her life in Moscow.

What had happened to her? Had her mother really been dying? No, I didn't believe that. The telegram had to have been a lie. It was just too much of a coincidence.

God forbid the very thought, but maybe Galina had been sent to prison? There was nothing I could do. I felt useless, hopeless, confused.

18

Moscow: 1977–1978

Galina kept writing, even though she was hearing nothing from Zambia. Either her letters or mine were not getting through. Whatever was happening to our mail, she knew the only chance we had of ever being together was for me to come to Moscow. She knew very well she was lucky to have a job, and appreciated how her new headmistress, M, was as helpful as she dared to be in the circumstances.

Most of the time she managed to stay cheerful. An optimist by nature, she did her best to convince herself that she would have her heart's desire some day, somehow. But there were dark times too, when she would dream of those idyllic days and warm loving nights in Africa, and wake in the small hours to find her pillow soaked with tears.

And some things were very hard to cope with. The nearest her public veneer of dutiful repentance came to cracking was the day she had to sit among her colleagues at the school and listen to a guest speaker bragging and swaggering about Russia's 'exemplary record of human rights'.

This speaker had been invited to the school to talk about a recent international conference in Geneva on the anniversary of the signing of the Helsinki Agreement. She had attended the conference as head of the stenographers' pool, so had been present at every session.

Galina heard this woman condemn, in the strongest possible terms, the way in which delegates from the Western countries had dared to reprimand Russia for violation of human

107

rights, particularly the right for Russian citizens to marry foreigners.

'What rubbish they threw at us, such lies their foul mouths uttered.' The speaker was incandescent with outrage. 'Of course our country honours the agreement. No other country has done more for human rights than we have. Everybody knows this. It's nothing more than another filthy Western lie.'

Galina had never felt so isolated. No one knew better than she did what lies this woman was mouthing. And everybody in the hall was applauding, believing these terrible untruths. She wanted to stand up and shout, 'What about me? What about my human rights?'

But she knew she must not say a word. She sat swallowing tears and clapping her hands like everyone else and thinking she might die, her heart was hurting so much. She could only console herself with the thought that at least she could confide in her friends, her true friends who understood her trouble and who would never betray her.

Her dear friends kept asking what had happened to her, and when she said she had been kicked out of Africa and told them the whole story, without exception they said, 'How can we help you?' This was true Russian friendship. When someone was in trouble, friends would rally round to offer support.

One friend said she knew someone who worked in the beauty parlour and who had as a client a woman in an important position in the Visa Department, OVIR. This friend introduced Galina to the beautician, Albina, who asked her to come next day to the beauty parlour. This particular beauty parlour was part of a cosmetics business in the centre of Moscow, and behind the scenes was a large laboratory where new products were researched and manufactured.

So Galina went to the beauty parlour at the appointed time and Albina rang the woman from the Visa Department.

'V, my dear, it's me, Albina. How are you?'

'I'm okay. And you?'

'Fine, thanks. My dear, why don't you come in this week? We have a wonderful new range of creams and lotions I know would be perfect for your skin, so delicate, so sensitive. You'll love them. We've also got an excellent new shampoo I'd really like you to try.'

'No, no, I'm sorry, I'm really very busy. I've got no time at all this week. It will have to wait.'

Galina could hear the other woman's replies. Albina smiled at her and said into the phone, 'Perhaps I can help? I have a friend here who has one or two quite little questions she would like to ask you. I could send her now, and she could bring some samples to you.'

'Oh – well . . . okay. Send her over.'

The beautician said to Galina, 'Take her a little "thank you" along with the samples. Nothing too big, you must start with something small.'

'I have a little African carving.'

'Oh, she'll love that, yes, give her that.'

So Galina went to the woman in the Visa Department and introduced herself, saying she had come from the beauty parlour. 'These creams are for you, and the shampoo.'

Galina handed over the package.

V asked, 'How much do I owe you for this?'

'Nothing. It's free. And here is a small gift for you, from my African trip.' She offered V the delicately carved little elephant she had bought at Lusaka airport.

'Okay, what is your question?'

'Marriage to a foreigner.'

'Who?'

'An Englishman.'

'What are the difficulties?'

Galina said, 'A Party reprimand. I was a Party member, and I was taken out of Africa for disgraceful behaviour.'

'Forget it,' V said. 'A member of the Party with a stamp like that on your record – there's no chance. You might as well forget it.'

'No, I can't forget it. I want it very much.'

'How much is very much?'

'I'm prepared to give everything I possess.'

'And what do you possess?'

Galina said she had *valuta* certificates.

'How much?'

'Several thousand pounds' worth.'

'Hmm . . . which is possible, maybe. What else do you have?'

'I have very beautiful furniture.'

The woman V tapped her desk with her manicured finger-nails, looking at Galina, considering. 'Give me his name and I'll try. First I need to check to see if he's on our lists . . . if he's clean with us.'

'Of course he's clean,' Galina assured her. 'He has never been to the Soviet Union. He doesn't know anything.'

'Don't be stupid!' The reply was scathing. 'We have so many names of people, we have people who have no idea they're on our lists. If someone mentioned his name, or he wrote an article in a paper, or someone reported something he did or said . . . Give me his name and come back in three days.'

Three very long days later, Galina returned to the Visa Department. V said, 'It's okay. I've checked, and he's not on any of our lists. Now let's go.'

'Go where?'

'To your flat, of course.'

'But why?'

'To see the beautiful furniture.'

They took a taxi to Galina's flat. V looked, touched, assessed. Then she said, 'Okay. Let's do it. But remember – there will only be one chance. Everything must be done the first time he comes. You will never get a second chance.'

Galina nodded. 'I understand.'

'So let's get started. You need to send him an invitation to come as your personal guest.'

Galina interrupted to exclaim, 'But it isn't allowed, to have a personal guest. Nobody can do this.'

V laughed. 'Nobody does it because nobody knows it's okay. The law allows it.'

Galina knew that what V was saying was probably true. As with so many things, those in the know kept their knowledge to themselves. If V was right . . . Peter would be able to stay in her flat, as long as he had the right papers.

V went on, 'Then you need to have a form written by him giving all his particulars, plus a completed visa questionnaire. You must tell him to be sure this is correctly filled in, all right?'

'Yes, I'll make sure he understands this.'

'You also need to collect all the necessary documents for yourself, permits from work, from the caretaker in your flat, from anyone else you can think of who might raise objections if you don't ask permission. Most of all, we need the documents from him. When you have all these papers ready, send them to me.'

After so many months of waiting, Galina realized there was no chance of anything getting through in the ordinary mail. She had to think of some other way.

She headed for the Central Post Office on Gorky Street. Trying to make herself as inconspicuous as possible among the people crowding the counters, she hung around picking up leaflets, pretending to read notices. After what seemed like hours, she heard two people quite close to her speak to each other in German. A man and woman, both young, they looked like students.

Making sure no one could overhear, she spoke to them casually in their own language. She chatted with them for a few minutes, asking what they thought about the beautiful things they had seen in Moscow, which of the historic buildings they admired most. . . . They seemed happy to talk to her, and in the course of the conversation they mentioned that they would be flying out to West Germany in two days.

It was now or never. She couldn't risk staying too long in the Post Office, lest she roused someone's suspicions. For all she knew, she might be under observation.

'Please – would you take a letter with you and post it in West Germany?' she asked them, dropping her voice.

The couple looked at each other. Obviously the request alarmed them.

Galina said, 'Look, this is the letter – it's only a love letter.' She opened the envelope. 'Read it. Please. It's nothing to anybody else, but it's so important for me.'

111

She hardly dared breathe while the students read the few lines on the page she handed them.

'Dear Peter,

'I am not coming back. My mother is OK, she was never ill. The only way to see each other again is if you come to Moscow as my personal guest. I will do everything I can here, but I need you to send the right forms completed, especially the visa form.'

Bless this young couple, they took the letter and posted it as soon as they got to West Germany. It reached me three weeks later.

19

I drove straight to Lusaka, to the Russian Embassy. Going through the procedure of admission brought back all too vividly the apprehension I had felt on my first visit. A person could disappear without trace, I had thought then. Had that been a premonition?

A different official dealt with my request to apply for a visa to visit Moscow. He pushed a sheaf of forms into my hands. I filled them in standing at the counter, and handed them back. 'We'll send you the documents,' the man said. 'It will take about a week.'

A week passed. Two weeks passed. Nothing happened. I went back.

'So sorry.' Yet another official. 'We gave you the wrong forms last time. Here are the correct ones. Fill these in, and it will all be okay.'

Another week. Another two weeks. Nothing. Back to the Embassy. My forms had been mislaid. Terribly sorry, fill in these others.

I realized what was going on, but I kept trying. Maybe, just maybe, they'd get fed up seeing me and let me have the visa.

I lost count of how many times I drove from Senanga to Lusaka and back. I lost count, too, of how often I got stuck and had to dig the Datsun out of muddy holes in the unmade stretch between Senanga and Mongu, the only route up to the metalled road to Lusaka. It was all for nothing.

Maybe the Russians had orders to prevent me travelling to

Moscow. Maybe they were just plain scared on their own account. After all, these people were responsible for their own nationals in Zambia. They were the ones who left Galina on her own in Senanga for months on end, and who took no action even when she was openly living with an Englishman.

I reckoned they saw her official disgrace as their own failure. Who knows, maybe they could lose their jobs, or even their liberty. It seemed a shade over-dramatic to think their lives might be in danger, but whatever their reasons, they were taking no chances. They were not going to help me. I had one last try, met the usual lies, and trudged over to the Lusaka Hotel, where I sat for an hour with a cold beer.

There was only one possibility left.

'It's a last resort, Kaye. I can't think of any other way.'

I had driven out to our old friend Kaye Townsend's house and talked the problem through with him. Kaye agreed that the Russians would go on doing everything they could to obstruct me.

'They won't refuse you straight out,' he said. 'They'll simply fob you off. Very politely, of course. I can't see any other way but to go behind their backs if you can. Better use the phone here – at least your call will be private.'

So I telephoned my mother. Over a line crackling with atmospherics I told her what was happening, or rather what was not happening. 'Can you get me some forms so I can travel to Moscow? Sorry about the bother, but the only way you can get what I need is to go to the Russian Embassy in London. I need papers to go as Galina's personal guest, and I need a visa form – that's the most important thing of all.'

On my way back to Senanga I made a short stop at Mongu to visit the hospital. I'd had a nagging toothache for weeks, but I'd put off doing anything about it. Like most people, I've never been overfond of the dentist's chair, but now it seemed wise to have the tooth seen to. If I did somehow manage to get to Moscow, I didn't want to risk having to see a dentist there. The less attention I drew to myself, the safer I would be.

This would be my first dental treatment of any kind outside the UK. My family had attended the same dental practice for years and I had a check-up every time I went home on leave, but on this trip I would only be in the UK long enough to pick up my papers. So needs must, I reckoned. *Courage, mon brave!*

The primitive-looking surgery did nothing to soothe my jumping nerves. Health care in Zambia was chronically under-funded, but even so, a good scrub-down wouldn't have done this place any harm. The dentist himself looked okay, though. His clean white coat and his wide friendly smile made me feel a shade more at ease.

I settled into the chair. Oh, Galina, if you could see what I'm going through for you!

The probe dug deep, and the dentist announced a cavity in an upper left molar. A simple filling should do the trick, he assured me. I've never been one of those macho types who brave the drill without painkillers, so I accepted a needleful of cocaine with gratitude and relief.

With the tooth drilled and filled, I drove on to Senanga to wait for news from England.

My mother got the forms from the Russian Embassy in London, no questions asked. She posted them to Senanga, I filled them in and sent them straight back to her. She then posted them to the Russian Embassy, as though the request were coming from within the UK. All the documents came through without the slightest hitch.

Why on earth had I wasted all these weeks yo-yoing between Senanga and Lusaka? If only I'd sat down and used my brains instead of dashing around like Action Man!

It was all incredibly easy, probably because the Russians in London were dealing with tourists and trade delegations all the time. And of course they had no idea they were giving a visa to someone intent on marrying one of their citizens.

I sent the documents in a registered envelope to Galina in Moscow. We had wasted an awful lot of time, but we had learned some valuable lessons on how to beat the system.

20

Moscow: April 1978

Things proceeded slowly, but they did proceed. Every negotiation with V from the Visa Department dug another hole in Galina's bank account. Every bit of help filling in Form A or Form B, every bit of advice, see this person, see that person, meant another trip to the currency shop.

In Galina's school, too, every question she needed help to answer, every form she needed help to complete, required a visit to the currency shop. She went to the currency shop so often, she felt her footsteps must be imprinted in the threshold.

V was actually a very pleasant woman but, as Galina soon realized, she did not have a happy home life. She was always pleased to have congenial company, and took a great liking to Galina. She invited her regularly to the theatre, and never seemed to have any problem getting tickets for even the 'sold-out' productions. V was good to Galina and gave her a great deal of help and support, even though her help always carried a price tag.

Getting things done through the back door needed patience, tact, and hard currency, but there was no other way. It was all proving very expensive, but if Galina expressed the tiniest doubt about the slow progress she seemed to be making, V was quick to reassure her that it was all going as well as could be expected, given the highly unusual nature of the enterprise. Slowly and patiently, that was the way to get things done. Any attempt to hurry the process could quickly arouse suspicion.

Albina's husband disagreed. He said, 'Why don't we fight this legally? The State has no right to treat you this way. The Helsinki Agreement permits marriage to foreigners. Our country signed it, and should honour it. Besides, you were brought back to Moscow by an act of deception perpetrated by the State, were you not?'

With the best of intentions, this man persuaded Galina to go with him to see a lawyer. The lawyer said she should forget it, there was absolutely no possibility of suing the State for deception. The State was not accountable to an individual citizen.

In fact, Galina did have a case. The Ministry, an agent of the State, had sent her a telegram saying her mother was dying, which was not true, and so had tricked her into leaving Africa. Surely this was deception? But Galina took the lawyer's advice to drop any thought of suing. She was afraid such an action at this time could destroy any chance of getting permission for me to come to Moscow. Better to go on visiting the currency shop.

21

Senanga, Zambia: July 1978

All I could do now was wait for my next leave. I thought about
packing in my job and trusting to luck, but quickly dismissed
the idea. I had been appointed Head of the Mathematics
Department only a few months ago, and very much wanted to
come back to Zambia with Galina as my wife. I had no money
to speak of, certainly not enough to support us. At least one of
us needed a job to come back to.

The day after term finished I drove up to Lusaka airport to
book my flight to London, the first leg of my journey to
Moscow. The next flight was three days away. I drove to Mongu
to spend a night at Brian's house, then went to Senanga to get
ready.

I could hardly contain my excitement, and rushed around
Senanga, telling all my friends I was off to see Galina at last.
Everyone was happy for me, and there was a lot of teasing and
joking. 'You're a brave man. The Russkis'll never let you out
of there once they get you in. You'll never come out alive. Who
do you think you are – James Bond? You look more like
Oddjob!'

In those days when East-West relations were far from cordial,
everyone, myself included, thought my trip was a great adventure. Many of my colleagues had travelled widely, but no one I
knew had visited Moscow.

Quite often in Zambia European families made friends with
families from the Soviet Union, and exchanged addresses with
them. Most Europeans were still naïve about the way things

118

were in the USSR, and fully expected to hear from their new friends and maybe even be invited to visit them. They sent letters, even gifts, but there was never any response.

'Why haven't they written to us?' they would ask Russian families still in the townships. These Russians must have known the situation, but didn't dare explain the silence. Russian families knew full well there could be no future in friendships with Westerners, but they could say nothing.

The jokey warnings ran off me like water. Nothing mattered now – I was high on adrenalin and joy. I went to our house to pack, and danced around the place singing, 'I'm going to Moscow, going to Moscow, going to see Galina . . .'

22

England: August 1978

I flew overnight to Heathrow, and by the time I nosed my hired car on to the M4 the rush-hour traffic into London was building up fast. It was August, and the summer sun was already warming up the day.

The Fiat 131 was a pleasure to drive, and its radio brought me the morning news programme crisp and clear. Nothing it told me meant very much. Perhaps I'd been out of the UK too long, but I couldn't have cared less about the latest strikes and political scandals.

On the approaches to the city the traffic got more and more congested and I got more and more tired and short-tempered. After the open roads of Africa, rough as they were, this fume-laden nose-to-tail crawl was quite literally hell on wheels.

I had phoned my mother the night before from Kaye Townsend's, asking her to contact Galina in Moscow to let her know I was on my way and give her the flight details. Had my mother got through? Would Galina be waiting when my flight touched down? Had she been able to make arrangements for our marriage? Would the Russians find anything wrong with my papers? Would it all go horribly wrong at the last minute . . .?

Questions chased each other around my tired brain on the long drag through London and up the A1 to Lincolnshire. I headed straight for Spilsby, where I knew my mother would be looking after my grandparents in the caring way she always did.

We'd always been a close-knit family, and for the last few

years a degree of guilt had come home with me on every leave. These two dear old people were in the twilight of their lives, and I knew very well they would love to see me far more often than they did.

My grandmother still struggled around their bungalow doing her chores in spite of the crippling pain of advanced arthritis, and my grandfather was fit and active and still driving his car in his mid-eighties. It struck me how much of my robust health and strong physique I must owe to them. My guilt was all the greater now, for I would only be under their roof for a few hours. My flight to Moscow was due to take off from Heathrow just about the time they would be sitting down to breakfast.

My mother told me about the problems she had had ringing Moscow. Galina had no phone in her flat, so my mother had to ring Galina's mother, Anna. Anna's flat was on the opposite side of Moscow, but Galina was usually visiting there around the time my mother was to phone. There shouldn't have been any problem.

As luck would have it, on the very day my mother rang Galina had gone out looking for wallpaper and paint, to decorate her flat ready for my arrival. Galina was teaching her mother the rudiments of English so she could at least greet me when we met, but as yet Anna's knowledge of the language was rudimentary, to say the least.

My mother's account of the 'conversation' didn't exactly fill me with confidence. She knew not a word of Russian, of course, so all she could do was shout down the line in English. A very poor line hadn't helped matters. The only words Galina's mother seemed able to pick up and repeat were 'airport', 'tomorrow', 'Peter', and the numbers two and five. What Galina's chances were of working out which flight I would arrive on, we could only guess and hope.

I dragged my weary body out of bed, showered, and forced down a piece of toast and a cup of tea. It was three o'clock in the morning. I felt absolutely shattered, but at least the roads in rural Lincolnshire were deserted, and the Fiat zipped along through the countryside. I was well on my way even before the tractors trundled out, and long gone before the tourists began to head for the beaches. The drive went so smoothly I got to Heathrow and boarded my plane with time to spare. But oh dear heavens, how tired I felt. Still, a good sleep on the plane should see me okay, I thought, and settled down to dream about seeing Galina again.

Had she got my message? Would she be waiting at the airport? If she wasn't, the only way to get to her flat would be by taxi. Would the taxi driver find her street, her building? Would the driver understand me? How could I even be sure there would be a taxi to hire?

I checked the piece of paper Galina had sent me with her address written on it. Another thought brought a fresh wave of panic. The address was an apartment block. It didn't give the number of her flat. How would I find her?

My hands were shaking, and I forced myself to take deep breaths. This was stupid. I'd hitchhiked around Europe, got by in Rome, Venice, Paris. I'd survived in The Congo, Kenya, Uganda, Tanzania, even the Kalahari and the most remote bush country. I had always been happy to have a go at anything. Why should I be afraid of a civilized city like Moscow? I didn't know why – but I was.

23

Moscow: August 1978

Galina decided her bedsitter badly needed redecorating. In the general shops in the city you couldn't buy anything very much, but she wanted to put up new wallpaper and paint the woodwork. At least that would freshen the place up a bit.

She spent fruitless days tramping the streets from one shop to another, one queue to another. In the shop that called itself, grandly, 'The House of Wallpaper', there was almost nothing to buy, yet you queued for hours even to get inside. The only wallpaper worth buying was a dark shade of red, a colour she didn't really like. But it would look better than the old paper, which had got very shabby.

She employed a woman to put the wallpaper up and do the painting. Then she cleaned the whole flat and made it as attractive as she possibly could. On the great day, she took a taxi to the airport.

Galina was waiting at the barrier, just as I hoped and dreamed. She saw me before I saw her, and ran into my arms. We hugged and kissed and hugged again. I could hardly believe we were together again at last, after so many months and so many traumas.

She had asked her taxi driver to wait. This was such a special day, she said, and she felt so good. As we rode into the city we couldn't stop looking at each other and touching each other's hands and face. We had waited so long for this, it was as if we had to keep reassuring each other it really was happening.

Before we went into the building where Galina had her flat, she said, 'Please, Peter, don't say anything while we are in the elevator.' It was best if people didn't know I was a foreigner, she said. Muscovites were not accustomed to seeing foreigners, and she didn't know how they would take it, my visiting her flat. She didn't tell me at the time, but what she was really afraid of was that someone might think my presence worth reporting to the authorities. She didn't want to take any risks.

Exhausted though I was, I could see how proud Galina was of her little flat. She had told me how most Muscovites lived, in large communal flats with whole families in one room and everybody sharing one kitchen and bathroom. She felt very privileged and lucky to have her own private place. She was very excited, and eager for us to go out together and celebrate. She had booked a meal with champagne at the Intourist Hotel, a very special treat. I guessed it was also a very expensive treat.

All I really wanted was to put my head on a pillow and sleep off the journey. I was so very tired and feeling far from well, but I didn't have the heart to disappoint Galina. She wanted to go out, it was all arranged, the taxi driver was waiting. ... So we left my luggage in her flat and went back to Red Square, to Gorky Street, to the Intourist Hotel for dinner.

Galina glowed with happiness. Her eyes shone and she couldn't stop talking and laughing. Caviar arrived, and champagne ...

Food and drink have always been among my greatest pleasures in life. This should have been my happiest day for a very long time, but I felt too exhausted to manage more than a glass or two of champagne. I could only pick at the caviar – what must it have cost Galina? – and pretend I was enjoying it.

We went home to the flat and got into bed. For more than a year I had dreamed of this moment, of making love to Galina again. And I couldn't. We held each other close, but my fatigue was so profound, so overwhelming, I couldn't make even a pretence at passion.

What a disappointment I must have been to Galina. We hadn't seen each other for such an age, but the only thing on my mind was sleep. Sleep, rest, time to let my body recover

124

from the driving and flying, then driving and flying again that had knocked the stuffing out of me. I couldn't remember ever feeling so shattered in my whole life.

I couldn't even find the strength to apologize. Nothing mattered . . . nothing but sleep . . . and sleep came quickly – but not for long.

A stab on my back like the prick of a sharp needle woke me all of a sudden. I moved and reached to scratch the offending spot.

Galina sat up. 'What's the matter?'

'A mosquito's got me!'

She switched on a bedside lamp. 'Don't be silly! There are no mosquitoes in Moscow You can't have mosquitoes on the fourteenth floor of a tower block.'

I jumped – another jab. 'I'm definitely being bitten. It must be bedbugs!'

Galina's temper was not at its best. Understandably. 'Look, I've just repaired and cleaned everything, top to bottom. We're not that dirty in Moscow! This is not an undeveloped country, with bedbugs everywhere.'

We switched on the main light and checked every inch of the bed, inspected every millimetre. No bugs. We switched the light off. Almost immediately I switched it on again. Something *was* biting me, I hadn't the slightest doubt. Something was pricking my skin, stinging me first here, now there. It felt as if an army of termites was eating its way over my body.

Galina had long given up any hope of a romantic night, and now here she was being accused of keeping a dirty home. She was a very unhappy lady.

We climbed all over, stripped everything off the bed again. Then Galina said, 'Look!'

She was pointing at my chest. I looked, she stared, and even as we watched, blisters like tiny boils erupted all over my skin, front, back, everywhere. We couldn't believe what we were seeing. Bright pink spots swelled up, blistered, opened and wept.

It was terrifying. I could only think it was exhaustion from the journey, and maybe stress from all the months of anxiety,

125

causing some kind of festering that was literally bursting out of me. I was very very frightened.

Somehow we got through the night. We lay awake into the small hours, not daring to touch each other, and eventually we both fell into a merciful sleep.

In the morning, things didn't look so bad. The rash was still there, but it had subsided a lot, and to my profound relief I was feeling a little better. We decided it must have been something I ate that had maybe caused a violent reaction, and my body had been too tired to fight it off in the normal way. In the early hours, as everybody knows, the smallest discomfort can seem like a nightmare. I pushed to the back of my mind the worrying thought that, in fact, I had eaten hardly anything. We felt a lot happier as we watched the sun rise over the rooftops of Moscow. At least, we convinced ourselves we did.

There was a great deal to do, and no time to waste. For a Muscovite to marry a foreigner, there was a complicated process involved, but at least it should be possible now I was actually here.

The first step was for me to visit the British Embassy, to inform them of my intention to marry Galina Vasilyeva, citizen of Moscow. The necessary documents would be filled in and pinned up on a special notice board in the Embassy. If anyone wanted to object to the marriage, they had to come forward at this time. It was a procedure rather like posting the banns before a wedding in England. Assuming no one raised objections, the documents would be handed over to me. Armed with these, we could then approach the other side.

Galina had searched out the only place we could get married, Wedding Palace Number One. The Russians required 31 days to issue the licence, and the queue for a slot at the Wedding Palace was long. All this palaver had to be got through before my visa expired. We only had three months. If we failed ... But no! We wouldn't fail. We couldn't ...

We took a taxi to the British Embassy on Maurice Thorez Embankment. Galina had never been inside any foreign embassy before, and she gripped my hand nervously when she saw the armed militiamen on the door. I showed my British passport and we were taken in straight away to see the consular, a young woman who greeted us with a smile.

The three of us chatted quite informally for a few minutes, and when I mentioned Zambia we discovered we had some friends in common in the Western Province. I could sense Galina beginning to relax. We filled in the required forms and were told to come back in three weeks for the affidavit.

Galina breathed a big sigh of relief when we came out of the Embassy, and we decided to walk a little in the morning sunlight. We strolled along by the Moscow River, looking across the water to the Kremlin, Moscow's 'citadel', with its onion-shaped golden domes.

Galina was looking forward to showing me around Moscow, she said, there were so many wonderful things to see. She was obviously very proud of her city. She began to tell me a legend about the Cathedral of St Basil, which we would see when we crossed the river. The cathedral, she said, was originally built for Ivan the Terrible and called the Cathedral of the Intercession. It was renowned far and wide for its beauty and splendour.

'According to this legend, when the building was completed Ivan the Terrible sent for the architects. He asked them if they would be able to build another cathedral as fine as this, or even finer. Yes, they answered, if they had the time and the right materials, yes, they could.

'When he heard this, Ivan ordered his guards to put out the men's eyes, so that no building more beautiful than the Cathedral of the Intercession would ever exist on earth.'

As Galina spoke I began to shiver, in spite of the sun's warmth. I could do without reminders of Russian ruthlessness.

Arm in arm we strolled across a bridge and walked through busy streets towards the nearest Metro station. The people we passed were dressed quite drably, but they didn't look as dour and downtrodden as I thought they would. Nobody took any notice of us.

We saw golden domes and silver domes, and we did see the Cathedral of St Basil, but I don't think I was very receptive to the beauty Galina said it was famed for. It seemed to me like something a child might have made with Plasticine. I could see no symmetry in its mixture of tent roofs and multi-coloured painted domes, and my tired brain couldn't make sense of its strange design. It looked as if Ivan the Terrible's unfortunate architects had never heard of proportion. I think Galina was disappointed at my lack of enthusiasm, but I felt too rotten to care very much.

But the Metro station ... Here was a different kind of beauty. Modern, functional, and clean. Spotlessly clean.

We bought our tickets, five kopecks to travel anywhere in Moscow. I laughed when Galina complained about the price. 'Well,' she said, 'it only costs three kopecks on the buses and the trolley buses and the trams.'

The station was immaculate. No litter, no graffiti anywhere. An escalator slid us smoothly down to the platform, and we stepped off into a marble palace, a gleaming cathedral. What a sight. Harrods' food hall without the food.

Every station I saw in Moscow was every bit as impressive. They were individually designed, and so clean, and there wasn't a speck of litter to be seen in spite of the crowds who used the underground every day. I wondered what on earth Galina would think of the London Underground, with its extortionate fares and its litter and grime, not to mention the graffiti that defaced every accessible inch of it.

We came up from the Metro into Kalinin Prospekt, a great avenue wider than any street I had ever seen in the West. Yet in many ways it felt almost as if we'd stepped back into Western Europe. There were flashing neon signs everywhere, reflecting their hard bright colours in the plate glass of modern shop frontages. I wouldn't have been surprised to see 'Coca-Cola' blinking its crimson message at the sky. I couldn't understand any of the signs, of course, and even when Galina translated them they meant nothing to me.

This, she said, was the first street of its kind built in Moscow, with skyscrapers and neon lights, as western as could be. Why the Russians should want Moscow to look like New York, the heart of everything they professed to despise, was beyond my

128

comprehension. Like Texas, everything had to be bigger, better and three times wider.

The lights came on in the shop windows as dusk fell quite suddenly. I saw crowds of people around what looked like a large supermarket. There were ranks of trolleys for putting your shopping in, just as you'd see outside the new self-service stores springing up everywhere in the UK, where you could wander up and down the wide aisles and help yourself from shelves packed with goodies.

The difference here was that the shelves were empty – except for tinned fish. Nothing but tinned fish. Tomorrow, Galina said, there might be no fish but plenty of potatoes. 'That is the way it is. You learn to live with it.'

You learned to live with it. Here in one of the world's greatest cities, you learned to live with food shortages even worse than I had coped with in a mud-hut village in the African bush. I could hardly believe what I was seeing.

I was still feeling under the weather, but we were so happy to be together that I tried to ignore the shivers that swept over me every few minutes. I was thankful there didn't seem to be any hint of that awful pricking rash.

We had walked around Moscow all afternoon. Usually I'm the model tourist, keen to see everything, the first to try any new experience. Today, it was an effort to put one foot in front of the other. Now it was evening, and Galina suggested we find somewhere to eat. This was not as easy as it sounds. Moscow is not at all like London, where you can find restaurants in every street in the West End and in nearly all the suburbs.

I didn't feel the slightest bit hungry, but Galina tried to persuade me I should try to eat something. 'Your body needs fuel,' she said. 'It will make you feel better.'

She took me to a back street and into a little bar she knew, and ordered something bland, I've never been able to remember what. I felt desperately tired, and every now and then a kind of dizziness would grip me, making everything seem far away and somehow distorted. Then it would pass and the world would seem quite normal again.

People around us picked up that we were speaking English, and came to our table to talk to us. Everyone was very friendly, and some of them knew a little English. They were all very interested, and got quite excited when we told them about our forthcoming marriage. Plates of food and bottles of beer kept arriving at our table.

At any other time I would have tucked in and thoroughly enjoyed both the food and the company. I was feeling really lousy, but I did my best to be sociable and not let Galina see how miserable I was.

The crowd got merrier – and louder. My head was ringing. Everybody had plenty of advice to offer about where we should go for a holiday while we waited for our marriage papers to be processed.

'Go to Sotschi, go to the Black Sea.'

'I have relatives there.'

'Who's got a pen, I'll write down some addresses for you.'

It was so jolly and kindly meant. In any other circumstances I would have revelled in the bonhomie.

24

Moscow: August 1978

We took a taxi home, and all I wanted to do was get to bed. By the time we got into the flat I was shivering uncontrollably. Galina found a thermometer and took my temperature. It was 102° and climbing. I was bathed in cold sweat, and nothing seemed to be making sense any more. The only thing I was sure about was that something was very badly wrong with me. This had to be something a lot worse than tiredness.

Poor Galina. She'd been waiting months for her ardent English lover. Now she had a sick sweaty shivering wreck on her hands.

By morning my temperature was 104° and the sweat was pouring out of me. Galina was terrified. I must have been pretty frightened myself, but most of those terrible hours are lost in a haze of confusion.

Galina insisted on going to see her doctor at the local polyclinic. From what she said, this sounded like a kind of general practitioner's surgery. I didn't like the idea. Galina didn't waste time arguing. 'You need a doctor. There's nothing else to do.'

The doctor came as soon as she could, but we had to wait nearly seven hours. She examined me, then took Galina to the other side of the room. I couldn't understand a thing, but I could hear angry words being exchanged. I could only lie there worrying.

Galina came over and told me what the trouble was. The doctor had accused Galina of letting her down by calling her out to someone who had just come from Africa and who therefore might be suffering from a contagious tropical illness. She was angry because her clinic might now lose some award or other, which depended on avoiding such things. They had had no such illnesses for several years, but now they might have lost the competition.

Surely that couldn't be right? Either my hearing had gone funny or Galina's English was not up to translating what the doctor had said. Clinics and doctors didn't behave like that – did they?

'I have to ring the Intourist Clinic near Byelorussia railway terminal,' Galina said. 'The doctor says I should ask for clinic number four. That's the clinic for VIPs, and for foreigners especially. They can't deal with a foreigner at her clinic.'

So Galina went out to phone this Intourist Clinic. 'You must bring a blood sample at once to the hospital,' they told her.

When Galina came back from telephoning, the doctor took blood from a vein in my arm. 'I'll take it over to the hospital myself,' she said. 'I'm sure they'll want him to go in.'

I didn't want to go. 'I want to stay here,' I said, trying to sound brave but feeling ashamed of my weakness. The idea of going into a Russian hospital terrified me. I had read plenty of spy stories. I knew what went on in Russian hospitals. They'd never get me into a place like that.

So we spent another night in the house. And what a night! I never want another like it as long as I live. I was sick all the time, retching hideously, though I had scarcely eaten a morsel for days. Galina had a terrible time trying to cool me down and keep me dry. She bathed me and changed the bed again and again till there was no more dry bed linen, no more table cloths, no more towels. She had no washing machine, so the soiled linen piled up in a corner.

Dawn had hardly broken when an ambulance arrived from the clinic for foreigners. Galina hadn't called it. She had been afraid to go out and leave me alone. The ambulancemen told

Galina that as soon as the hospital had the results of the blood tests, they sent for me. I had to go. No arguments.

Imagine how I felt. Feverish, sick and exhausted, I was already in a sweat. This ambulance was taking me to a hospital in a city where I was living in highly unconventional circumstances, to put it mildly.

Galina had resigned from her job. People had talked to us in the hotel, in the bar. There were eyes and ears everywhere in Moscow, I knew, because Galina had told me often enough, and I had raised a few eyebrows at the airport by refusing Intourist's offer of a hotel room. Did they have a dossier on me already?

Through the streets of Moscow we rushed, blue lights flashing, sirens screeching like banshees. Consciousness came and went as the miles stretched between me and the only person in the world I wanted to be with. The only person I loved. The only person I knew in this alien city.

My memories of arriving at the hospital are vague, to say the least. I remember being stretchered through a door in the wall of a building and hearing a clang just like the sound of the Russian Embassy door in Lusaka shutting behind me a lifetime ago. I stared up at a stark white ceiling only a few feet square. Were we in a lift? The next thing I remember is waking up with a nurse bending over me.

25

Moscow: August-September 1978

I could see a toilet in a corner, and a bath. The plumbing was
exposed, its paint peeling off in layers. I counted seven shades
of grey. I could see them quite clearly.

There were needles taped in the back of my hand and two
bottles of fluid hanging above my bed.

No one could speak my language. The faces of the doctors –
all women – showed no emotion. There were dozens of them
round my bed, swaying to music I couldn't hear. I passed out
again.

The nurses came infrequently, and when they did I never knew
whether to feel glad of their company or afraid of what they
were going to do to me. There was always an injection,
sometimes two or three. I wanted to ask that they were drip-
ping into me, but I didn't know how and I felt too weary to
bother.

The colour of my urine was horrible. Terrifying. What poison
was at work in my body to produce such vile waste?

The hours dragged by. Often I lay awake till dawn, too
scared to go to sleep in case I never woke up. The parting
words of my friends in Senanga came back to haunt me through
the long nights. 'You'll never come back alive.'

Most frightening of all, I didn't know what was wrong with
me. Galina said the doctors wouldn't tell her. And I couldn't
ask.

*

I was semi-conscious for nearly a month. Galina visited the hospital every day and stayed as long as the doctors allowed. She can describe those terrible weeks a lot better than I can.

'They took Peter to the Botkin Hospital. This was a special hospital for contagious diseases. As soon as I knew he was going there, I guessed what was wrong with him. He must have hepatitis. Botkin was a Russian doctor in the nineteenth century. He specialized in the diagnosis and treatment of hepatitis. In Russia they called hepatitis "Botkin disease".

'I followed the ambulance in a taxi. Peter was admitted at once to an isolation ward on the ground floor. You couldn't walk straight into this ward, you had to go through a door into a very small ante-room where there were facilities for changing your clothes and washing your hands. Then you went through a second door into the ward. A similar arrangement on the opposite side of the ward allowed access from the main hospital.

'Peter was in a special wing for foreigners. I was allowed in to see him from the very beginning, but I had to come in from the grounds and go through the ante-room procedure, wash my hands and put on a white gown.

'He was not in a general ward, he had his own room. I had never seen anything like this before, a room in a hospital for just one person, what a luxury. It wasn't a large room, but it had a high ceiling and very tall windows, looking on to the hospital grounds.

'None of the doctors or nurses could speak a word of English. I had to translate everything for Peter. He was drifting in and out of consciousness, sometimes quiet, sometimes shouting in delirium. Now and then he would open his eyes, but I don't think he really saw anything. His eyes looked absolutely awful, sunken in heavy red rims. The whites had turned a dirty dark yellow colour, and the skin on his face and his body had gone yellow now too. His urine was almost black, and his excrement chalky-white.

'The doctors put him on drips immediately. He was so obviously an emergency case, they worked very fast to get the intravenous tubes into place and operating. Dr Valentine, the

135

consultant looking after Peter, told me they had diagnosed serum hepatitis.

'They gave him a diet of boiled cabbage without salt. He pushed it away, said he couldn't eat. I think maybe it was that he didn't want to eat the cabbage.

'At the end of a week he lapsed into unconsciousness. The doctors said there was nothing I could do, just wait. I should go home and get some sleep. After a sleep I would be better able to help him if – if! – he came round again.

'I did as they told me. I didn't want to leave Peter, even for one night, but I didn't want the doctors to say I was a nuisance and maybe not let me in again.

'I went home and collapsed. Next morning when I went back Peter was still unconscious. I sat the whole day beside his bed, and the nurses brought me food. One of the nurses said to me, "He is dying, you know. He will not recover. Let him go home, let him go to England. Let him die in England."

'I tried not to listen to this. I had great faith in this hospital. Russian medicine has always been very fine, and apart from this nurse the medical staff at the Botkin were confident people, very sympathetic.

'"Oh, poor Englishman," they said. "He came to get married and landed up here. But if he has hepatitis, this is our speciality. We will cure him, don't worry."

'From the moment Peter regained consciousness he held my hand. My heart ached for him. He tried not to let me see it, but he looked so scared. This great big strong man lay there so weak and helpless, not able to understand what was going on.

'I had no connections with Peter's Embassy. All the documents for the marriage, all the telephone numbers, had been given to him. We had not had any time to discuss the arrangements, and now he was in no condition to do anything. If we were going to get married before his visa ran out, it was up to me now to get everything organized.

'It was even more important to find some food that might tempt him to eat. I found what I could, even watermelons and bananas. He asked me to get Ribena and Coca-Cola, things that could not be found in Moscow.

136

'Doctor Valentine was very supportive, and I really think Peter owes his life to the good care she gave him. After a few days he began to shout at her a Russian phrase he had picked up from the nurses, *"Yah hauchew yeast!"* – "I want to eat." That he had found the strength to shout anything seemed like a miracle, and my hopes began to rise.

'The only thing he was willing to try to eat was mashed potato. He wouldn't even taste any of the Russian food I offered him. So mashed potato it had to be.

'Every day, I made mashed potato in the morning at home, wrapped it up hot in a blanket, jumped into the back of a taxi and took it straight to him in hospital. My flat was quite near Baumanskaya Metro station, but you can imagine it would not be too easy carrying hot mashed potato on the Metro.

'So two or three times every day I travelled back and forward by taxi, cooking mashed potato and taking it to him, from one side of the city to the other. The journey took about forty-five minutes each way, but all the effort seemed worthwhile when I saw him eat my mashed potato.

'The hospital had a shortage of nursing staff, so I had often to take Peter to the toilet, change his bed, sponge him down . . . all the non-medical duties I could take from the nurses' shoulders. I was very happy to do this, to help Peter get well again.

'None of the nurses knew any English. One of them came to me and asked "Can he speak Russian?" I said no, he couldn't. "Oh – poor thing!" She couldn't believe anyone existed who couldn't speak Russian.

'We had to let Peter's Embassy know what was happening. They were expecting us to continue the process of arranging the marriage, but we had dropped out of sight. One day Peter told me, "Contact the Embassy," but I didn't think I could. I was very scared of going there. I didn't like dealing with officials, especially foreign officials.

'It took me several days to find the courage to get the phone number from Peter. It seems like such a simple act, to ring the British Embassy, but it filled me with fear and trembling.

'I rang Peter's mother and told her what was happening. She

was very worried, of course, even though she could have no idea how seriously ill Peter really was. I told her about his desire for Ribena and Coca-Cola, so she rang the Foreign Office in London and managed to arrange for me to pick up some drinks from their Embassy in Moscow. This must surely be the longest distance order ever for a Coke.

'So now I had to do it, I had to actually go to the British Embassy, to collect the drinks for Peter. I set off, absolutely terrified. It must be difficult to understand, for anyone who has not lived under such a system as ours. All Russians gave these foreign embassies a wide berth, and here I was having to find the nerve to go inside one on my own.

'Our last visit here was such a happy time for us, setting in motion the formalities of getting married. It was so different for me now.

'There was an armed militiaman on the gate. He was a Russian, of course. There was always at least one of these armed guards at the doors of every embassy in Moscow, and their job was to stop any of us Russians going in there. The Soviet Union did not want any of its people getting in to ask for political asylum.

'"I approached the militiaman and presented my bravest face. He asked me "What are you doing here?"

'"I have come to collect drinks for my friend."

'"Who is your friend?"

'"My personal guest – an Englishman."

'"Which hotel is he staying in?"

'"He is staying with me."

'"That cannot be."

'"He is staying at my flat, as my personal guest . . ."

'This argument went on and on, but I refused to go away, and at last he gave way and let me pass. I didn't get any drinks that day, but they said if I came next day the drinks would be ready for me.

'I didn't want to go through all that again, so I rang the Embassy and they very kindly delivered a crate filled with bottles of Ribena and Coke to the hospital.

'Peter got his Ribena and his Coke, but I vowed never to go

to the Embassy again, I felt so scared. To us, embassies were like fortresses. To go in was absolutely not allowed.

'Anyway, I had told the Embassy of Peter's condition, and I believe his mother informed them too. They hadn't known he was in hospital. The hospital was under no obligation to advise anyone about their patients.

'Things happened very differently from the way they were in England. I could not have contacted his Embassy if Peter hadn't given me their telephone number. In Russia, there was no public access to telephone numbers. There were no such things as telephone directories.

'As soon as the Embassy learned Peter was ill, they informed the hospital they were sending a young lady Consular to see him. What a metamorphosis took place! There was much scrubbing of walls and floors, dusting everywhere, changing curtains, fresh flowers appearing all over the place ... they worked all day to make the place more than presentable, it was like preparing for a royal visit.

'When the lady Consular finally arrived, she wore a summer dress that had seen better days, and flip-flops on her feet. It was obvious to me she had decided to burn them all after her visit, this was such a serious disease. She told us her name was Miss Stirling, and she sat as far away from Peter as she could get.

'Out of Peter's hearing, she told me she had been given gammaglobulin injections before she came, as serum hepatitis had a sixty per cent mortality rate. She advised me to fly Peter home to England. Then she asked Peter if he wanted a priest. They didn't have one at their Embassy, she said, but they could make an arrangement with the Americans who they knew had one.

'Peter said "No! No priest!" He sounded so angry I knew he must be feeling a lot better.

'He had to sign an affidavit for the marriage. Time was passing, and his visa wouldn't last for ever. He must get this step out of the way before we could go any further.

'Miss Stirling agreed to come again and bring a Bible so we could complete the formalities in Peter's room. We needed this affidavit badly. All the procedures must take place from the hospital.'

When the Consular arrived next day I was feeling much better. I had managed to eat and drink a fair amount the evening before, and didn't feel quite so frighteningly weak.

Miss Stirling brought the Bible as promised. She also gave me a pair of thick yellow gardening gloves to put on, so I wouldn't contaminate it.

I stood up in hospital pyjamas as least three sizes too small for me, despite the huge amount of weight I had lost. With one yellow-gloved hand in the air and the other on the Bible, I quoted the required words from the Good Book, prompted every now and again by the Consular. She, too, wore rubber gloves and held the Bible with her fingertips, keeping her body as far away from mine as she could without falling over.

The Botkin was a teaching hospital, and whether by design or coincidence Dr Valentine arrived with a party of students. They stood behind the glass observation window, gaping at the proceedings. What must they have thought of these idiotic British with their quaint rituals?

I was improving rapidly now, and beginning to think I might be well enough to go back to Galina's flat. I was off the drips and eating reasonably well.

Then one morning, on what seemed at first to be a routine visit, Dr Valentine suddenly produced a dictionary and announced: 'Knife . . . cut . . .' With her forefinger, she drew a line from my throat all the way down my torso. There was no language barrier here.

'*Niet*! Absolutely *niet!*'

At that moment Galina arrived. Doctor Valentine spoke to her, talking very fast and making extravagant gestures. Galina took my hand and said, 'The latest tests are not looking like the classic hepatitis picture. Nobody is sure any more that it *is* hepatitis, but they don't know what else it might be. We must pray for hepatitis – they know how to treat that.'

The doctors kept Galina out of my room for the next day or

two, till they knew exactly what they were dealing with now. For two whole days she spent hours at a time standing outside my window so I could see her and know she was there for me.

It was at this time she noticed a militia car drive into the hospital grounds and park close to the outside entrance to my room. She didn't tell me about it till she had watched it come and go over a whole week.

26

Moscow: September 1978

They took me for an X-ray. This was my first time out of that depressing room for well over a month. I was managing the few steps to the toilet and back to the bed quite easily now, but walking all the way to the X-ray area made me feel horribly shaky. Standing at the X-ray machine I felt sick and faint, and thought I was going to collapse. I was very glad to get back to my bed. I climbed thankfully on to the hard mattress, realizing there could be some time to go before I would be up and running again.

When it was time to prepare for my operation the doctors relented and let Galina back in, mainly, I think, so she could calm me down and explain what was going on. They calculated my weight, so they could work out how much anaesthetic to give me. When Galina translated the weight they read off, the figure was nearly six stones less than the scales usually registered. That meant I was now less than two-thirds the man I had been.

Dr Valentine asked me about allergies, then they got me ready for the operation. Apparently, this was nothing like as serious as I had imagined. They were going to do a laparoscopy examination of my liver. It was hardly major surgery, but I still didn't fancy it, and kept saying, "*Niet! Niet!*"

The consultant got fed up with this and gave us an ultimatum. 'Okay,' she said, 'there's a plane waiting. We don't want the responsibility of not doing everything we can for him. We certainly don't want a foreigner dying on us, so if he doesn't agree to the laparoscopy, that's it. We have the medical plane ready to fly him home.'

Galina sat on my bed and held my hands. She said, 'The choice is, if you go home on the plane you might not be able to come a second time, but it's now a question of your life. Forget about marriage, it's not important now. You must go home, you must go on the plane.'

That was no choice at all. I said, 'I want to stay with you. I won't go. They can do the laparoscopy.'

The usual theatre was undergoing repairs, so they had to take me to a different part of the hospital. They walked me along corridors, then we passed a couple of theatres where operations were going on. They parked me on a seat outside my theatre. Another operation was in progress and while I waited my turn I couldn't help seeing what was being done to the lady on the operating table. You can imagine what this did to my nerves.

Galina was still with me, gowned up, and she asked a man behind a desk if I could sit somewhere else. With considerable relief, we followed him round a corner to another corridor.

Eventually my turn came. I clambered on to the operating table and a doctor gave me an injection in my arm. My worries drifted away. Galina was holding my hand, and nothing else seemed to matter any more. The surgeon arrived with his team, and they began to prepare their instruments. This was too much for Galina. She gave me a kiss and beat an understandable retreat.

I came round on a trolley in the corridor. Galina was there, holding my hand and still in the gown and mask, swamped by white linen and looking like a novice nun. I was so glad to see her.

She held on to my hand and made little shushing sounds, but I soon sensed something strange about her. She didn't seem able to look into my eyes for more than a second or two. Something was wrong. I felt it in her fingers, saw it in her eyes. Galina was worried. Why?

Two orderlies carried me through my ante-room and placed

me on my bed, grumbling all the time. 'They are saying you are such a big heavy man,' Galina said. If only they knew. A nurse made me comfortable, and I must have fallen asleep.

When I woke, Galina was sitting by my bed and her face was a tight mask of anxiety. As soon as she saw my eyes were open, she smiled brightly and began to chatter. The nurse had said I couldn't have a drink yet, even if I was thirsty, it might make me sick, but I was not to worry, I would feel much better soon and the doctor was coming in a minute and everything was going to be all right . . .

I could feel her hands trembling in mine. Something terrible had happened. Or something terrible was about to happen. Should I ask her? Or wait for her to tell me? I couldn't decide.

Then Dr Valentine arrived. Immediately, Galina jumped up and took hold of the doctor's arm talking low and fast. Was she afraid I might understand what she was saying? I lay there watching, unable to move.

Dr Valentine left the room. 'What's wrong?' I asked Galina.

'Wrong? What could be wrong, my darling? We are all looking after you. Doctor Valentine has to see to something, that is all.' She laughed, a light lilting laugh that rang in my ears like a cracked bell. 'Nothing is wrong, we are waiting for your results. You must rest now. I will stay here with you.'

I wasn't going to get another word out of her till the doctor came back. I was still woolly from the anaesthetic. Whatever the trouble was, it would have to wait. I surrendered to sleep.

The sound of voices work me. Doctor Valentine was back. And Galina was smiling. The biggest, broadest smile I had ever seen on her face. Even in my dazed state I knew it was genuine.

'It's okay,' she said. 'Doctor Valentine says it's hepatitis B with Australian antigen.'

The doctor smiled too, and indicated she would come back later. When she had gone I said, 'What's so wonderful about hepatitis B with, what did you call it, Australian antigen – or whatever?'

'Hepatitis B with Australian antigen. Hepatitis is very

144

common in Zambia. You must have picked up the germs in Senanga. It's a very dangerous kind of hepatitis. One of the worst, Doctor Valentine says.'

That dentist in Mongu! That must be it. I remembered the friendly dentist in his dapper white coat. Not much point in a clean white coat if his instruments were dirty. He must have been re-using needles without sterilizing them properly. Damn the man! I'd have him sacked when we got back.

Well, it might be small consolation, but at least we knew for sure it was hepatitis. I'd survived this far, so I was probably going to live. 'But why were you so worried?'

'Ah ... well, you see ... You remember the operating theatre you were in .. ?'

'I'm not likely to forget it.'

'Well ... when I came back – I had to rush to the toilet, I was so frightened for you my stomach turned to water – when I came back I asked a doctor who came out of the theatre were you nearly finished and what did they find out ...?' She had turned quite pale at the memory. '... and this doctor stripped off her gloves and threw them in a bin and said without looking at me, "Cancer of the pancreas." These were her words, "Cancer of the pancreas, in the last stages." And she walked away. She just walked away and never looked at me.'

'My God! What happened then?'

'I could do nothing, only wait and pray. I believed you were dying. I was numb with fright. We got you back here to bed, and you fell asleep. I ran to find a telephone to ring my mother. I asked her to find out all about cancer of the pancreas, and she said she would ring a friend who is a doctor. She said I must wait half an hour and ring her again.

She was gripping my hands so hard it hurt. 'I rang again and my mother said no, it couldn't be like that, they can't say things like that without a biopsy. They have to do a biopsy, and they have to confirm the results. From a laparoscopy operation, they can't know for sure if it's cancer or not.'

She smoothed my hair and kissed me. 'I told Doctor Valentine what the other doctor said, and she said no, they haven't said anything like that to me. She went to check for me. That

145

was the worst two hours of my life, my darling, waiting for her to come back.

'That's what she was telling me, just now. The cancer of the pancreas was in the other theatre. It was all a terrible mix-up. You've definitely got serum hepatitis, not cancer of the pancreas. Oh, I'm so happy I could sing – if I could sing!'

And we laughed together like a couple of fools, happy that I only had hepatitis, not cancer. Only hepatitis! Still, we tried to look at the positive side. If I hadn't come to Moscow, I might already be dead. The Botkin Hospital and the Russian doctors saved my life, no question about it.

As the days passed and my strength slowly built up, Galina began to bring me books to read, mostly novels. At first, I found it difficult to concentrate for more than five minutes at a time, but gradually my concentration improved, and reading became my favourite way of coping with the time when Galina couldn't be with me.

That stark little room with its dingy walls and peeling pipes ... I tried not to picture how different it would be at home with get-well cards all around and friends bringing flowers and grapes and bottles of Lucozade and orange squash...

I read the only two English language papers available, the *Morning Star* and the *Moscow News*, but these were boring in the extreme and so predictable. Some factory or other was exceeding all expectations and producing more goods than ever before ... British police were bullying the poor downtrodden workers again ... the Americans were up to more dirty tricks...

I was very grateful for the few books in English Galina was able to find, *Doctor Zhivago* by Boris Pasternak, Solzhenitsyn's *The First Circle*, the terrible story of Myra Hindley and the Moors murders, a couple of Agatha Christies ... Galina got the Solzhenitsyn and the Pasternak from friends. Both of these books were banned in the USSR.

One book in particular fascinated me, and I believe it played a big part in preserving my sanity. This was Henri Charrièrre's *Papillon*, the true story of a man imprisoned for years on

146

Devil's Island. In comparison with what happened to Charrière, my life in the Botkin Hospital was paradise. He spent years in solitary confinement, never allowed even to talk to anyone. I couldn't communicate with anyone at the Botkin when Galina wasn't around, but at least the people who looked after me were not hostile. My physical conditions were blissful compared to what he had to endure.

Charrière's story was an inspiration. It made me realize the value of taking a positive attitude, and gave me strength to tell myself I was going to get better, I was going to beat this illness and make a complete recovery.

I tried not to worry about the militia car, which was still making regular appearances.

My ultimate aim now was for Galina and I to get married. Although I still found it hard to accept the need to stay in hospital, the days didn't drag quite so wearily now I was thinking more positively. Galina kept me as well supplied with reading material as she could, and we often played cards. As my concentration improved, we began to play the occasional game of chess.

Now I was taking an interest in life again, she told me how all her friends were asking about 'Our Peter' and sending good wishes. I had met L and his wife in Lusaka, but hadn't met any of the others yet. I hadn't even had a chance to meet my future mother-in-law.

Galina never once failed to appear at my bedside in the mornings. How she had the patience to put up with my grumbling and complaining I'll never know, but she was always cheerful, always confident that I would make a complete recovery. If there was ever a test of our feelings, it was those weeks in the Botkin Hospital.

27

Around this time, Dr Valentine told Galina an American had arrived in the hospital. He was in a ward not far from mine and, according to the doctor, was feeling desperately lonely. He had travelled through India with a friend, and on their way back to the States they decided to spend a few days in Moscow. They stayed in a hotel, and he became so ill he was admitted to the hospital. His friend had to leave him there.

I sent him a book and a note, introducing myself and wishing him well. A few hours later a nurse brought a letter from him. 'Dear Peter,' he wrote, 'your letter was like a ray of sunshine to me . . .'

His name was Neal Grace, he wrote, and he was a philosopher and a poet, and he was also a vegetarian. Poor fellow, I thought, he must be having a tough time. There was no such thing as vegetarian food in a Russian hospital.

He was locked in his ward, and sat on a window-sill all day reciting poems about philosophy to people as they passed. They didn't understand a word, just stopped and stared at the mad American. He was hungry, he wrote, hungry for poetry and hungry for food. He couldn't eat anything, he didn't know what was wrong with him or how long he would have to stay.

'I'm paying one hundred dollars per day for my treatment and medical expenses, and I'm still having to pay for my hotel room in the city. I am absolutely broke and I don't know what to do.' This shook me to the core. I had been here for six

148

weeks. It didn't take long to work out what an enormous sum I was going to have to pay.

When Galina arrived later that day, she found me determined to leave the hospital. Four thousand dollars plus was an awful lot of money. And I had no insurance policy to cover sickness abroad. (I've been a lot more careful about taking out adequate cover since then, I can tell you.)

Galina had some money, but most of what she had left was in roubles. The Russian authorities wouldn't take roubles. They insisted foreigners pay in hard currency, and Galina had spent a great deal of her hard currency already, on 'favours' for the many people who had helped us. We had to conserve what was left, in case more problems came up, requiring more favours.

My imagination was working overtime. I'd be a headline in *Pravda*: 'British teacher defrauds Moscow hospital ...' I'd be banged up in the Lubyanka ... 'Bring my clothes,' I said. 'We're leaving.'

'You can't leave,' Galina was firm. 'You are not well enough yet. And that car is outside again.'

When Dr Valentine came on her regular visit in the late afternoon, Galina mentioned my concern about money.

'Don't worry,' the doctor said, 'he's lucky, he's an Englishman. There's a reciprocal agreement between Russia and Britain. Treatment is free for British people here, and it's free for Russians in Britain. There is no reciprocal service with America, so they have to pay in full. I am not going to let Mr Young out till his bilirubin reading is low enough. The risk is too high.'

Galina translated, and I calmed down a lot. When Dr Valentine had gone I said, 'What on earth is bilirubin?' I'd never heard the word before, and didn't like the sound of it one little bit.

'It's nothing serious. It's all part of the same illness. It means there are some red-coloured particles in the bile. Don't worry, it's getting better.' I hoped she was right. It sounded very nasty.

149

I never did get to meet the American, Neal Grace. He discharged himself after a few days.

I was beginning to get really agitated. I was feeling so much better now, and couldn't wait to get out of this place. The doctor would say, you can go next week, but when next week arrived the bilirubin hadn't dropped enough, so then it was 'next week' and 'one more week'.

Then one day Dr Valentine came to say it was okay for me to take a short walk. Galina was to come with me. 'Not too far. Half an hour at the most.' Fantastic! Galina and I went through the ante-room into the hospital grounds, and for the first time in weeks I walked out into the fresh air. It was dry and sunny and quite cold, but I was well wrapped up and didn't mind the nip in the air. That first stroll, short as it was, showed me how weak I still was. It felt great, just the same.

'There's no sign of that car,' I remarked as we came back into the grounds.

'It won't be back,' Galina said.

'What do you mean?'

'It won't be back. I mentioned it to L. He said, don't worry. It's not a problem.'

'What's L got to do with it?'

She shook her head. 'Poor L. His wife has left him, you know. They haven't been getting on since Zambia.'

I vaguely remembered Galina mentioning that L worked quite close to where she lived. They had been friends for years, and he often visited her place. What did the militia car have to do with him? I tried again, but Galina would only say, 'Don't worry about it.'

We never saw the car again.

The first signs of winter arrived with dropping temperatures and light flurries of snow. Galina walked with me every day, and soon I could just about amble as far as the Moscow Dynamo stadium, round the corner from the hospital grounds.

We were all still watching the colour of my urine. Slowly, very slowly, it was returning to something near normality. To this day, if I eat or drink anything out of line, my urine reflects my sin in its darkened colour. It's as though my water is trying to say: 'Steady on, lad. Remember Moscow. You don't want that again.'

28

Moscow: October 1978

While I was stuck in hospital, Galina was making approaches to the Russians about our wedding. She went to Wedding Palace Number One, the only place, as I've mentioned, where Russians were allowed to marry foreigners. This was the same wedding palace where Christina Onassis had married Sergei Kausoff only a short time before, apparently unaware of his KGB connections. I remembered reading about this in the papers, but I hadn't taken much notice. I would have been a lot more interested if I'd known I would be getting married myself in the same Wedding Palace.

Galina went through all the usual channels, all the normal procedures, and was told the waiting time for the marriage of a Russian to a foreigner was one month minimum. We only had a month before my visa would expire. The usual channels were no good to us.

Galina went to her friend Albina the beautician, and explained the problem. 'Don't worry! Don't worry at all! The woman in charge of Wedding Palace Number One also comes to my salon . . .'

So once again Galina took the creams and the shampoos Albina parcelled up for her to give to the woman in charge of the wedding palace.

This woman was ill at the time, and was lying in another hospital, so Galina had to go and see her there. She sat at the woman's bedside and explained our predicament. We couldn't wait a month. My visa was running out. I would have to leave without marrying her ... there would never be another chance.

'No problem!' the woman said.

It wasn't free, of course. Favours never are. The woman wanted jewellery, a gold chain, a crystal necklace and ear-rings. So Galina took her precious currency roubles to the *Beryozka* shop and bought the best she could find.

We had our licence in less than a week.

I was getting more and more fretful. I've never been a patient man at the best of times, and I've always hated inactivity. This confinement was shredding my nerves.

I had been in the Botkin Hospital for more than eight weeks when at last Doctor Valentine let me go. She stressed that she was giving me permission to leave only on condition I came back every day for tests and treatment. The hospital would not hand over my certificates of fitness until the prescribed treatment had been completed. I needed those certificates. Without them, the Zambian authorities would not allow me to teach in their country.

Galina had already sent a telegram to my headmaster to warn him about my late return to school. I wanted to go back to my job, especially now I'd been promoted.

While I stayed at Galina's flat waiting for the all-clear, her mother came to visit us nearly every day. From the first time we met, she insisted I call her Anna, and we got on tremendously well. Galina had been coaching her so she could understand and speak a little English, and she loved to practise her new skill on me.

I met some of Galina's most trusted friends, too, and found their company congenial and very stimulating. Most of them knew some English and some were quite fluent, so there wasn't really a language problem.

L spent a lot of time with us. He was looking for company, Galina explained, now he was living alone. We had Zambia in common, so we had plenty to talk about, and we got on very well. He had given Galina a great deal of support over the weeks I had been laid up in hospital, and I was grateful to him for that.

I had time to watch a bit of Russian TV, which was quite an eye-opener. Galina translated for me, but she didn't need to. The pictures said it all. Most of the news reports centred on Western Europe, and all too many of them showed police holding back crowds at some industrial dispute or other, with plenty of cleverly edited shots showing how the British police were 'constantly bullying the workers'.

The film-makers seemed to seek out the dingiest and most run-down surroundings they could find so they could show the Russian people how terrible conditions were for the workers in the UK. There was never a city park or a beautiful building or a well-stocked shop to be seen. Could this be my country they were talking about?

Our wedding day was approaching, and we were having difficulty finding anyone willing to stand as a witness. Galina was not surprised or particularly disappointed about this. People were scared for their jobs, she said, you couldn't blame them.

When she asked her friend V from the Visa Department, however, the answer was a confident 'Yes! I don't care. It's all legal anyway, you have permission, so why should there be a problem?'

Then at the last minute, one of Galina's former students came forward, a girl she had got very friendly with. So our small party was complete: Galina and myself, Galina's mother, our friends V, Olga and Yuri, Nina and Basil, Albina, Lucy, another friend called Olga, our young witness, and L.

By one of those odd coincidences, we were to be married on 24 October, which happens to be Independence Day in Zambia.

On the big day, we arrived at Wedding Palace Number One at the appointed time. We found we had to wait outside till our turn came. Couples waited in front of us, more couples fell into line behind. At last our names were called and we were ushered into the wedding hall, where an official shot questions at us.

'Do you want an orchestra or taped music?'

Galina translated for me. We decided to have taped music.

'Do you want champagne or ordinary wine?'

'Champagne,' we said.

'Do you want a photograph or not?'

This was getting silly, I thought. Of course we wanted a photograph. We wanted a keepsake of the occasion, so we could look at it and remember our wedding day. It was what people usually did, wasn't it? I said as much to Galina.

She whispered in English, 'Not always so, here. We must ask our friends if they mind being photographed.'

In my eagerness to get on with the ceremony I had forgotten that some of our wedding guests could be taking a risk merely by being here. Several of them decided they would rather not have their presence on record. I realized then just how fond of Galina they must be, to have come to her wedding at all.

It seemed an age till everything was arranged and the wedding began. The ceremony was conducted by a woman who wore a red ribbon and spoke in Russian throughout. Unreasonably, I felt quite disappointed at not being able to understand a word of it.

We stood under the hammer and sickle and listened to a solemn declaration which Galina translated for me afterwards: 'According to the law of the Soviet Union you are becoming husband and wife, you have to work for the State, you have to be a good citizen and show good moral behaviour.'

Nobody asked me anything.

There followed a very tedious 10 minutes of pompous Russian music, during which we signed a register and our witnesses signed too.

We were served with Soviet champagne. Though it's nothing like the real thing, this is actually very drinkable, and very cheap. I was only allowed a thimbleful.

We had our photographs taken, and my passport was stamped: 'Married to Galina Vasilyeva on 24 October 1978.' And that was it. We had done it.

We left the wedding palace, making way for the next couple in the queue. It was all so clinical, I hardly felt anything had changed.

155

We took a taxi back to Galina's flat, and sat holding hands as we hurtled along the boulevards. It didn't seem quite real. One thought kept going round and round in my head. 'You know,' I said, 'I never even said "I do".'

The day before our wedding, Galina had taken me to the *Beryozka* shop, where I bought hams and whole salmons and cakes and many other luxuries that were unobtainable in the ordinary shops. I paid for all this with my foreign currency, as Galina was not allowed to buy food here, even with her currency roubles. For food purchases, hard foreign currency only was the rule.

We had already assembled this multitude of goodies on the table in Galina's flat on the morning of our wedding day, and invited back the friends who came to our ceremony. Other friends joined our celebration, those who had been too nervous to put in an appearance at the wedding hall in case someone reported them.

I remember this gathering with tremendous warmth. For so many years East and West had been trying to outface each other in a Cold War that threatened the very existence of the human race. Yet here in this flat in the centre of Moscow, in the heart of 'enemy territory', everyone treated me like a dear friend. Galina's mother and all her friends accepted me immediately, and wished us every possible happiness in our marriage and in the new life we hoped to make in Zambia and eventually in England.

I looked back over the months I had spent in this city, and couldn't think of a single moment when its people had shown me anything but courtesy and friendship.

It was a happy convivial occasion, except that I could eat very little of the rich food, and couldn't drink at all. Can you imagine it, your own wedding and you can't eat the wedding breakfast or drink the toasts? It was a day I would certainly never forget.

Our wedding night was not so memorable, I have to confess. My physical state was simply not up to it, if you'll forgive the pun. But it was bliss, none the less, to cuddle close and talk in the warm peaceful darkness.

'We've got plenty of time now,' Galina said.

'I know. Isn't it marvellous?'

'I've never felt so happy, And I don't only feel happy, my darling Peter,' she said. She snuggled closer. 'For the first time I can remember, I do not feel alone. With you, I feel safe. Absolutely.'

I stroked her hair and caressed the soft smooth skin of her cheeks, her throat. I thought my heart would burst with happiness.

'You'll never be alone again, I promise. We're together now, for always.'

We could just about dare to think ahead now, to talk about our life together and make plans for the future. We were married at last, and we felt wonderful.

My visa had almost run out, and I had to leave Moscow. I wanted desperately to take Galina with me, but in Russia things were never that simple. We were legally married, but she was still required to apply for permission to join her husband abroad. She could not leave yet. I would have to return to Zambia alone.

To do that, I had to get booked on a plane. This sounds very easy, and in almost any other country in the world it would be – but not in Russia. I had more or less slipped past the authorities, thanks to Galina's contacts. I did not have the necessary permission to fly out. For British tourists visiting Russia, all the arrangements and all the bookings in and out were made in the UK in advance.

When I turned up out of the blue at the Intourist office in the Metropole Hotel, the girls behind the counter didn't know what to do with me. They just stared at me, mesmerized. At least they spoke English, though.

'We don't sell tickets to individual foreigners,' they said. 'We can't do this.'

'But where else can I go? This is the only travel agency in Moscow. I have to get on a plane, my visa is running out.'

After a lot of arguing, they agreed to phone around and see what they could do. They were quite suspicious of me, and kept coming back to check my passport and Galina's name and address, then going off to the phone again. But eventually they gave up, and issued me with a ticket on a BEA flight to London the next morning.

'Please be ready, Mr Young, and have all your papers with you. Our car will come for you to the address you've given us at seven-thirty sharp, to take you to the airport.'

Apparently I was being given the status of a foreign tourist, despite the fact that they'd never heard of me till today.

Galina and I made a last trip together to Wedding Palace Number One to collect the photographs of our wedding, the wedding we had feared might never take place.

But here were the colour photos we had posed for. There we stood, our little party, in a formal line-up, Galina very smart in a tailored suit, me looking half the man I'd been in Africa . . . me sliding Galina's wedding ring on to her finger, Galina and I signing the register . . .

Early next morning, with reluctance and with great sorrow, I got ready to leave. As Galina and I came out of the building, we saw L waiting there with Galina's mother in his car. I was very touched to find that several other friends had also gathered outside, all wanting to come with us to the airport. They were not going to let me go, they said, without a proper send-off.

Waiting outside, too, was the promised Intourist car, a very impressive-looking Zis. The driver loaded up my bags and Galina and I climbed in, followed by our small party of friends. We set off, L following on with Galina's mother. We streaked along the boulevards in the middle lane, the lane reserved for official vehicles. Everything gave way to us. If I hadn't been so sad I might have enjoyed it.

From Heathrow I flew on to Lusaka the following day, picked up the Datsun, and drove straight to Senanga. I walked into the staffroom and said, 'Would anyone like today's paper?'

There was a chorus of 'Yes, please.'

I threw down a copy of the *Daily Telegraph*, an early morning edition I'd picked up at Heathrow. It was only a small tease, but my friends' amazement delighted me. It made me feel I was getting back to my old self.

My headmaster called me over and said, 'Get back to your class as soon as you like ... they all love you and they've missed you.'

And I thought, Yes ... and there's someone 5,000 miles away who loves me even more.

29

Moscow: February 1979

It took four months for Galina to get permission to leave Moscow. This seemed like an age to me, but she thought it was pretty good by Russian standards. Some married couples waited for years.

Galina had to turn for help once more to V, her friend in the Visa Department. V was very happy to do this last service for her, and gave Galina the necessary forms and showed her how to get everything done in the shortest possible time. There were still a considerable number of signatures to get before Galina could obtain her passport and visa in her married name.

Things were a little easier for her now she was not working, but she still had to be registered with the Party, and she had to have a place of residence, an address to give the authorities. She didn't want to simply give her flat back to the State when she eventually got permission to leave the country, and she was worried, too, about what would happen to her mother, who was living in very basic one-room accommodation. The best solution all round, as far as Galina could see, would be to exchange her flat and her mother's room for one bigger flat.

They managed to find a couple who were divorcing and who were happy to move into the two separate places, freeing their two-bedroom flat on the outskirts of the city. Galina moved into this flat with her mother. When Galina eventually left, her mother would be comfortably settled in a flat of her own for the first time in her life.

Her domestic arrangements sorted out, Galina took her Party

card and went to the local municipal committee. Somehow, she charmed them into signing the necessary papers before they realized what they were letting themselves in for. There was a very hot exchange of words afterwards, but she didn't care any more. She had the Party signatures she needed.

She took the papers to the Visa Department, and was told to come back for her passport and visa in a few days. She was also told that the man who would be signing her documents wanted a mohair scarf, a small parting gift. So off Galina went to the *Beryozka* shop, but there were no mohair scarves to be found there. She tried all the *Beryozka* shops in Moscow, but none of them had a single mohair scarf in stock. 'There's no demand for them this year,' one shop manager told her.

Here was one demand, she thought, as she went back empty-handed to the Visa Department. Please could this man settle for something else? After some minutes of negotiation via a clerk, the official agreed to accept a pair of shoes, 'Size eleven, black, all leather, no laces, and they must be English.'

On the appointed day, Galina arrived at OVIR and the transactions took place. The official got his shoes and Galina got her foreign passport and her visa. They shook hands, and the man wished her all the very best in her new life. From the look in his eyes, Galina was convinced he would like to change places with her.

She thought about all the people who had helped her, who had helped us both. So often, bribery was the only way to get what you needed in life, yet people still managed to form friendships and to feel compassion. There were no bad memories, only gratitude.

The time came to say goodbye to V, who had given her so much help and who had stood so willingly as a witness at our wedding. Galina instructed a removal company to strip her old flat and take her furniture to V's address.

'I want you to have it,' she said. 'If it wasn't for you, I could never have married Peter. It's the only way I can thank you.'

'I'm not going to refuse,' V said. 'But it was good experience for me. I might be able to use it some day.'

Galina knew V wanted to arrange an emigration, not for herself but for her daughter. V had confided how she cherished the hope that her daughter would meet a foreigner one day and make a better life for herself in some other country, preferably Britain.

'Maybe one day I'll be able to help you,' Galina said, and embraced her friend.

Galina was flying to England, then almost immediately on to Zambia. Her luggage allocation was very small, so she concentrated on packing things for Africa, lightweight clothes, furnishing cotton for upholstery, cutlery, a few electrical gadgets, and of course all the wedding presents her friends had given us.

Most of the presents were souvenirs of Russia. There was a beautiful samovar, crystal vases and drinking glasses, ornamental plates, painted wooden spoons, etchings of Moscow scenes, *matriyoshka* dolls ... treasures to remind Galina of her life in Moscow. She wrapped each item separately and packed everything in strong cardboard boxes, tying cloth around them for extra protection. It was a long journey, and things could get badly damaged if they were carelessly packed.

As was customary, Galina had to bring everything except her hand luggage to Sheremetyevo Airport several days in advance, for checking. With her ticket, she had been given a detailed list of items that were allowed and items that were not allowed to be taken out of the country.

She looked on helplessly while the airport officials opened every box. They took out every single item, threw everything on the floor of the Customs Office. They unscrewed the iron. They took the radio to pieces. She watched in horror as the pile grew. It was an absolute mess.

The men found nothing. They said Okay, they were accepting her luggage for transit. 'Put it back,' they said.

She couldn't move. She didn't know where to start.

'We can do it for you – for a price.' The offer was made in casual friendly tones. There was no animosity, no coercion.

The price was far too high, but Galina said, 'Do it.' With the skill of professional housebreakers, they put everything back, wrapping the boxes in special protective covering material, even putting a metal band around the baggage.

Galina owned nothing very special, nothing out of the ordinary. But she had heard the stories about families who were leaving for America, and especially for Israel, having all their precious possessions deliberately destroyed, fur coats slashed, china smashed to pieces, pictures sprayed with obscenities. All this was done after people handed in their luggage and before it was loaded on the planes. Who could they complain to, when their vandalized possessions arrived on the other side?

Galina's days in Russia were coming to an end. Soon she would be flying out to England, to my country, where my mother and stepfather would be waiting for her at Heathrow. They understood their new daughter-in-law's apprehension about arriving alone in a strange country, and had promised to drive down from Lincolnshire in plenty of time. They would wait at the Arrivals barrier holding up a board with her name on it, so she should have no trouble recognizing them. They would see her safely on to her flight to Zambia. The arrangements were all in place.

The last day came, and Galina's mother and her closest friends came with her to the airport to see her off. They made quite a large party in the airport lounge, Galina, Anna, Nina and Basil, Olga, Lucy, Albina, and L. It was a Russian tradition to send a friend off with champagne toasts for future happiness and the beginning of a new life. Everyone was quite emotional, and wished Galina *Bon voyage* knowing they would probably never meet again.

For some reason that Galina could never figure out, this enthusiastic send-off seemed to offend the young women at Customs Control. One of them came over to her and said, 'That's enough! It's time you were on your way. The plane is not going to wait for you.' Her voice and manner were far from friendly. Last kisses and hugs were exchanged, promises made to write and to visit each other. Then with a last embrace for her mother, Galina walked through to the customs check.

163

The cold-eyed woman customs official searched Galina's hand luggage thoroughly, then took her into a side room and body-searched her. Every item of her clothing was closely examined. Every pocket was checked.

The official waited while Galina dressed, then said, 'Take off your ring and your ear-rings. They are diamonds, and they are over the permitted value.'

Galina was horrified. 'But this is my wedding ring,' she protested.

'I'm not interested in what it is. You know the rules. The only jewellery you can take out of the country are pieces worth less than two hundred roubles. These are worth a great deal more than that, and you know it. You can't take them with you.'

Time was getting tight and Galina didn't want to argue, so she took off her diamond ring, the ring I had put on her finger at our wedding. She took off the ear-rings that matched the ring. She had bought them with the last of her currency roubles as an investment to take with her to her new life, a little bit of personal security. She handed the jewellery to L, who was talking to one of the women at Customs Control.

'Please, L, give these to my mother. Ask her to keep them safe for me.'

She kissed him, and he put his arms around her and held her close in a warm hug. 'Goodbe, Galina,' he said. 'Good luck.'

She went through Passport Control. The controller was a military man, uniformed and armed. He looked at Galina's photograph, then looked at her. For a full minute he stared at her, his eyes hypnotic, unblinking, as if he were trying to read her mind. Then he waved her on. She walked through the gate and on to the airfield. The Aeroflot plane waited, a thin stream of people trickling towards it.

Galina was halfway to the plane when she heard someone behind her, running, shouting. 'Stop immediately.'

She turned round. One of the women from Customs Control was racing after her.

'Turn out your pockets!'

'What's the matter? You've already checked them.'

164

'Don't argue with me! Just do as you're told.'

So Galina put her hands into the pockets of her coat. To her astonishment, there in her left pocket she found her ring and both her ear-rings. The customs official took hold of her arm and pulled her hand out of the pocket. Galina stared, horrified, at the jewels that lay in her palm. They sparkled and shone, cold and brilliant in the evening sunlight.

The woman gripped her by the arm and marched her back through the gate and into the departure lounge.

The interrogation began.

'You tried to smuggle diamonds out of Russia.'

'No, I did not! I had no idea they were in my pocket. Absolutely no idea. I did not put them there.'

'Do you think we're stupid? We saw everything.'

'Then tell me what you saw,' Galina answered, 'for I saw nothing. Please – take these wretched diamonds. I have to get on this plane. My mother-in-law will be waiting for me in England.'

'Don't tell us what to do! You've been caught smuggling jewellery and you'll be dealt with accordingly. Tell us the truth.'

Galina insisted again and again that she knew nothing, that she had handed over the diamonds to her friend to give to her mother. How they got into her pocket she didn't know, had not the faintest idea.

There was a party of military men in one corner of the lounge, guarding a consignment of ammunition. One by one they drifted over to find out what the argument was about, and each one who came was a rank higher than the previous one. They seemed very interested in what was going on. They'll accuse me of smuggling guns next, Galina thought.

After much discussion among the customs officials in voices so low she could only catch an occasional word, she was taken back to Customs Control.

L, he to whom she had entrusted her jewellery, was talking and laughing in a very friendly manner with the customs staff. He took Galina's hand in both of his, and said it was all his fault, it was because he felt sorry for her. When they were saying goodbye and he thought nobody was looking, he had slipped the ring and the ear-rings into her coat pocket. It was a spur of the moment thing, a crazy impulse to help a friend.

'I'm so sorry,' he said. 'It was a foolish thing to do. Please forgive me. You are my dearest friend, and I only wanted to help. I thought you would need them for your new life. I wouldn't harm you for the world.'

To this day, Galina doesn't know the full story behind this. She knew L's parents both worked for the KGB and that he had done some minor work for them in Zambia, small things like recording the numbers on the licence plates of people visiting the British High Commission, or allowing his car to be used by Russian officials who didn't want to be spotted in places where they shouldn't have been. What he was playing at with the diamonds Galina didn't know, and she decided it was probably better not to know.

She was told she could go, but by this time her plane had taken off. She was very concerned about my mother, and what she would do when she realized Galina was not on the scheduled plane. She pleaded with the airport officials, 'Please, can you send a message to London, to Heathrow, so they can make an announcement to say I will not be on that plane? My mother-in-law will be waiting for me. She will be worried.'

But nobody wanted to know. They had already told her she could go, what more did she want? She was lucky not to be charged with smuggling, she should be grateful. Her problems were no concern of theirs.

Looking very contrite, L helped Galina book a seat on the next plane to London, the early morning flight, then he drove her back to the flat with her mother. She had three hours sleep, then got a taxi to the airport. She left her wedding ring and her ear-rings with her mother.

An official passed her through Customs with a casual wave. Once again, she walked through the gate and across the airfield towards the waiting plane, trying not to hurry, trying not to show how frightened she was, and all the way half-expecting to hear a voice shout 'Stop'. As she walked, she thrust her hands

166

deep into her coat pockets, terrified she might somehow find the diamonds there. She knew she would not dare relax till the plane was airborne.

She had splashed out on a first-class ticket, to travel in the style her new freedom deserved. To her disappointment, she found herself alone in the first-class section of the plane with nobody to share her triumph.

And it really was a triumph. She had scored the ultimate victory over the system. She had got out of it. She had won! She wanted to shout it aloud to the whole world.

Galina was on her way to England, to freedom. She was flying out to the husband she loved.

EPILOGUE

Kent, England: August 1984

The letter from the British Intelligence Service arrived in July 1984, two years after Galina and I finally left Zambia and came home to settle in England. I had taken a party of pupils to a schools' computer camp in the Lake District, leaving Galina alone for the first time since we had been home in England.

It had come to the notice of the service, the letter said, that we might have some information which could be of use to them. Could we please phone to arrange a meeting?

Galina sounded frantic on the phone. Weren't we finished with all that? What could the British Intelligence Service possibly want from us? Who were these people? M15? How could we be sure they really were who they said they were?

The short answer to the last question was, we couldn't. We had gone to Moscow on holiday in 1980, to visit Galina's mother. We'd had problems with Galina's papers, and I'd had to enlist the help of the British Embassy to get us out of the country again. Was this some kind of follow-up from that? I rang the number Galina read out over the phone and made an appointment for 28 August, at our home.

In his smart dark suit, with his black leather briefcase and his impeccable manners, our visitor reminded me of our friends at the British High Commission in Lusaka. He introduced himself as Mr Smith.

'We have a file on every East European living in the UK, but we don't have a file on you, Mrs Young.' He smiled apologetically. 'You've been missed, somehow. We need to ask you a few questions. It's very good of you both to give us your time.' Did we have any choice, I wondered?

Mr Smith wanted to know everything about Galina and about her associates in Zambia. How did she and I meet? Was she a member of the Communist Party? What did being a Party member involve? Where had she been in Zambia? Whom did she know in Lusaka? Did she come across the KGB? Who were her bosses in Zambia?

Mr Smith seemed perfectly happy for me to stay, but directed all his questions at Galina. I decided I would only speak if Galina got distressed. It was better to let her handle things as she thought best.

I sat looking at a picture that hung on our sitting-room wall behind the chair where Mr Smith sat with his legs elegantly crossed. An artist friend of Galina's had drawn this picture for us. Over dinner one evening we had got talking about my stay in the Botkin Hospital, and he was so intrigued by what had happened to us there, he drew one of the scenes as we described it to him. There I was in too-small hospital pyjamas, with my hands encased in yellow gloves, one in the air, the other on the Bible.

I looked at it now, remembering that terrible time and listening to Mr Smith's quiet voice questioning Galina. However polite it sounded, I knew an interrogation when I heard one, and I sat wondering if we would ever be left alone.

The 'few questions' took nearly two hours. Mr Smith was very thorough. As he prepared to leave and stood up to shake hands with us, he said, 'By the way, do you still have the letter we wrote you?'

Yes, I said, we did.

'Would you mind awfully getting it for me?'

I fished the letter out of a drawer. Mr Smith folded it and put it in his inside pocket.

'Thanks very much. You won't mention any of this to anyone, will you? As far as anyone outside these four walls is concerned,

169

this conversation never took place. I've never been here. Do you understand?'

We understood. We'd had plenty of practice.

Mr Smith picked up his briefcase, smiled, and left. We stood together and watched him walk away down our quiet road, the man who had never been here.